WOODHILL ROAD

Stories from the hardware store

Joe,
enjoy!!

Joel Madden

Also by Joel Mader

Cleveland School Gardens

WOODHILL ROAD

Stories from the hardware store

Joel Mader

abbott press®

A DIVISION OF WRITER'S DIGEST

Woodhill Road
Stories from the hardware store

Abbott Press books may be ordered through booksellers or by contacting:

Abbott Press
1663 Liberty Drive
Bloomington, IN 47403
www.abbottpress.com
Phone: 1-866-697-5310

ISBN: 978-1-4582-0649-7 (sc)
ISBN: 978-1-4582-0648-0 (hc)
ISBN: 978-1-4582-0647-3 (e)

Library of Congress Control Number: 2012920247

Printed in the United States of America

Abbott Press rev. date: 11/01/2012

For my beloved James Henry Bennett Jr.

CONTENTS

I would like to thank my editor, Charles Tuhacek. He kept me on track throughout every phase of the book.

A special thank you to my wife, Jacqueline, for her encouragement during the difficult writing times.

 Introduction

Cleveland, for most of the twentieth century, was a city of well-defined neighborhoods. To go outside your neighborhood was to go to a strange place. To travel as little as a mile in any direction could place you in a world of different languages and customs. The neighborhood was safe. Children could play on the streets and in the schoolyards without fear. The neighborhood was warm. People knew their neighbors and cared about them. Everything and everybody had its place. The merchants sold their goods in small shops on the main streets. The professionals—the doctors, dentists, and lawyers—would nestle their offices next to or above the merchants. The workers went to their jobs in the mills and factories within walking distance of their homes. The women stayed home to raise the children. Churches were the center of the neighborhood. People spoke of living in the Buckeye, Woodhill, and Kinsman areas around St. Benedict's church. The neighborhood was proud. The commercial buildings had the names of their owners etched in stone above the entrances. A person's every need was met in these enclaves called "the neighborhood."

The Woodhill Road community is located about three and a half miles southeast of Cleveland's Public Square. The total area of the neighborhood is a little more than a mile and a half square. This was a Slovak community. The Slovaks settled in this area during the great Slavic immigration period, as early as 1880. One of the merchant districts of this enclave was on Woodhill Road. The street was a mixture of factories, a public transportation yard, and small stores. The storefronts were reminiscent of Edward Hopper's painting *Early Sunday Morning*. The painting depicts a row of storefronts with apartment suites above. Like the painting, each store had large plate-glass windows and a sign.

For more than half a century, the Woodhill Road community was the home of common people going about their common lives. They were a common yet peculiar people because of their Slavic ancestry. They came from a country that never had an identity of its own. When the Slovaks came to the shores of America, they felt a freedom they had never realized in the old country. They longed to be part of a nation they could call their own. They told their stories of America—how they would have it better in America—to their children. They shared their stories at home around the dinner table.

They told their stories at church picnics and festivals. Lastly, they shared their stories with one another at unusual times in familiar places. Mader Hardware on Woodhill Road was one of those sharing places.

Chapter 1
MADER HARDWARE

Seldom would you catch a woman in the store. If a woman did come in to buy something, it was because her husband sent her with a drawing of a particular plumbing or electrical problem. Some of the funniest moments in the business were when a lady would present a drawing of pipes and a list of items needed. Usually the husband didn't really know what he needed, and his descriptions could have been in Sanskrit for all the help they were. The guys, our storytellers, would gather around and try to figure out the drawing. They would never embarrass the lady. When she left, they would almost pee their pants with laughter. They would talk of male and female fittings and couplings. The male fitting goes into the female coupling. What size nipples did she need? Was it close nipple, a copper nipple, an iron nipple? And all that talk of fluxing. They could hardly hold back with all the wink-winks and nudge-nudges. The average age of these old farts was seventy, but you would never know it by the way they talked. Every time they opened their mouths, the little boys in them came out.

The storytelling would start after everyone got comfortable; this usually meant opening their lunchboxes if they were factory workers and reviewing what their wives made for them that day. The professionals of the group bought their lunches at the local deli. On special occasions, John would have a pot of beef soup simmering for all to help themselves. A hot plate on the back bench was the makeshift kitchen in which John's delicacies were prepared. For those who wanted, there was a bottle of Black Jack underneath the back counter next to the turpentine. Cups were not needed; just wipe the top off with your shirtsleeve before and after taking a drink. If water was your drink of the day, a cold-water faucet, located behind the basement door in a cubbyhole, was available.

After these preliminaries were attended to, someone in the group would usually start off by saying, "You should hear what happened to me today." What was related was a mundane incident about his job, usually revolving around his boss. Another would tell how much worse it could be: "If you only walked in my shoes." Then the litany would start, always beginning with, "You think *you* have it bad?" This banter ended with one person prevailing by capturing the floor and beginning his tale.

Chapter 2
THE HEAD

"You think that's bad? You should've been with me the night I was pulling an eleven-to-seven as a Fourth District Cleveland cop back in 1954," Charlie said. Charlie was a WWII veteran. Back then, as now, police departments liked to snatch up veterans. They make the best cops. You don't have to train them as much. Charlie had been in the marines.

"It was about two a.m. I was sitting in my squad car thinking about the fight I'd had with my old lady that night, just before I started my shift. I called her a whale because, well, she plumped up forty pounds after a year of marriage. She got so mad, she threw the only thing that was handy—a statue of the Virgin Mary. Hit me right in my shoulder. To this day I can feel the pain. I got out of there fast."

"You and your old lady are always fighting," Milos said.

"Go to hell," Charlie shot back.

Milos and Charlie were good friends, but you would never know it by the way they talked to each other. They would meet a couple times a week with the group at Mader Hardware on Woodhill Road around noon just to "chew the fat." The hardware store was an old, traditional retail store. Big sign above the plate-glass sectioned window; Mader Hardware and Sherwin Williams—"The Paint that Covered the World"—wrestled for space on the sign. Old, never updated "sale" signs were taped all over the windows. Keys, two for thirty-five cents, were made. Paint thinner cost forty-eight cents a gallon. Brooms, mops, and clothes poles in a metal stand almost blocked the doorway. Gallons of paint were stacked in a pyramid outside. A handmade sign read "Special: Porch Paint, $1.50 a gallon." John Mader, the owner, made the paint himself by mixing sample cans in a big barrel in the back of the store.

The group would all stand near a radiator grate in the floor in the back of the store. John recently converted the coal furnace in the basement to a gravity air gas furnace. It wasn't as cozy as a potbelly stove, but it suited the purpose of bringing everyone together in one spot. In the summer, they would hang out back where Joel, John's son, would fix the windows and screens. Joel was the *sklenar*, which is Slovak for "window maker."

"Well, like I said, I got the call at two a.m. It was a bad night. A cold front came in around midnight. It was soup out there. The day started out hot. The temp hit ninety-five degrees. The clouds seemed to cough, and bingo! the temperature fell forty degrees. In July, mind you. Everything got murky. Dew sheeted my windshield. You had to use your wipers every few seconds. You couldn't see nothing until it was on ya."

"Shit, Charlie, you can't see nothin' on a clear day!" said Karol. Karol had just walked in from the factory for lunch. Today John had a pot of soup on for the boys from Weldon Tool. It was Weldon Tool's twenty-fifth anniversary of its opening. Whiskey too! The bottle was stashed under the counter next to the turpentine.

"Saw your wife the other day, and I wished it was foggy," Charlie snickered.

Karol raised his hand toward Charlie as if to smack the grin off his face, smiled, and reached for the whiskey.

"Seems," Charlie continued, "that some civilian heard a loud, crashing, metal-on-metal noise in the field across from the car barns down by Manor Avenue. He called the police, and I got the call to check it out. I know the area well. Kids play down there a lot. The railroad recently put up stranded wire rope across the access road down by the hill to keep kids and their cars out."

The teenagers in the neighborhood called it the Field. It was a place where they could go to play "capture the flag," make stinkweed bows and arrows, smoke, neck, and generally have a good time. Shit Creek was at the bottom of the hill, rightly named because of the sulfur, rotten-egg smell that came from it. Companies in the area used the creek as a catchall when they puked up their chemical waste. At the end of the creek was a pool. The area of the water was the size of a large spring pool that you would come across in woods. The depth was unknown. The chemical mix was like acid and seemed to eat through the layers of earth down to its core.

One of the favorite pastimes of the kids in the neighborhood was to try to find the depth of the pool. The foolish kids with handkerchiefs or snot rags over their noses and mouths would poke with long tree limbs into the putrid mess. They could never reach the bottom, but they never gave up. The creek and its pool had become a legend. If you wanted to go straight to hell, just dive into the pool. Railroad tracks ran alongside the creek. To get to the Field you had to cross a cinder parking lot. The Field was nothing more than a railroad siding with an access road down a steep embankment. The older teens would drive their cars down the road, find a place off to the side, and neck.

"Well, like I said, the fog was so thick you couldn't see nothin'. Try to use your high or low beams, didn't mean a thing," Charlie continued. "I pulled into the cinder lot about five miles an hour. Got out of my unit and slowly walked down the access road for about a half mile. I came up to right about where the steel wire rope should have been. Flashlight on. Didn't matter, couldn't see a foot in front of my nose. Bam, I walked smack into the back end of a car."

"Kids necking?" interrupted John. John had just come out from behind the cash register to hear Charlie's story.

"Yeah, that's what I thought too, but there was all kinds of debris on the trunk of the car. Still can't see. I felt around. I reached down and found myself holding a piece of the wire rope that was used to block the road. It was warm, almost hot to the touch. Wet and sticky too! I wiped my hands on my pants and poked around some more. Hanging from the wire was a piece of heavy cloth. At first I didn't know what it was, but then I realized that it was a top of a convertible."

"Hell, Charlie, did the convertible hit that wire rope?" Milos asked.

"Yeah, and I realized what happened at that instant. I carefully put my hands on the trunk of the car and started to make my way to the driver's side."

At this point in Charlie's story, stillness came over the store. Even the paint mixer suddenly stopped.

Charlie continued. "I heard a moan come from the passenger side so I reversed and slowly went around the back of the car again. I tripped and fell, broke my flashlight, and landed on what I would eventually recognize as the continental, the spare tire holder, of a 1954 Ford convertible. It was lying off to the driver's side. I crawled on my hands and knees, continuing along the other side of what was left of the car. Things were all tangled. The canvas top was pushed off to the passenger side. I worked my way through the mess and reached up to the car door handle. Suddenly a hand grabbed my hand and wouldn't let go. I almost shit my pants."

"Was it the passenger?" Karol asked as he threw back a shot of whisky straight from the bottle.

"Yes and alive, but I will never know why. It was a female, and she was pretty beat up. I felt her warm, bloody head with my other hand. It was smashed in on one side. I could feel her scalp was torn back and an ear was missing. This was not the movies. She kept moaning, 'Where's Jim … where's Jim?'"

"The driver," someone blurted.

"Yeah, the driver," Charlie answered.

"I got free of her hand and got up and quickly made my way back to the squad car. I called it in. An ambulance was on its way. It was too late for the girl. She was dead by the time I got back to her.

"I worked my way around the front of the car. The hood was hot. It didn't seem to be damaged. Headlights were out. Slowly, I inched my way around to the driver side. I got to the driver's door and reached in and felt a shoulder. The driver. *Feel for a pulse,* I thought. I reached for where I thought his neck would be and my hand fell into a warm, liquid, slimy cavity. I immediately pulled my hand back. No head. He'd been decapitated. He was sitting upright, hands on the wheel as if driving. A modern headless horseman."

"What'd you do, Charlie?" someone asked.

"Pissed my pants, that's what. I was covered in blood. The car was covered in blood. Both of these kids had bled out all over the car. Here I am alone next to this kid without a head." Daylight would reveal fragments of pallid, purple, pale flesh everywhere.

The group looked at each other, then at the floor, then at Charlie, and then at the floor again. No one said a word.

"My backup finally pulled up. The fog lifted to reveal the extent of the accident. The car hit the wire rope at full speed. There was no sign of braking. The rope peeled the convertible top back and off to the side. The girl passenger was slumped over. Dead. What was left of the driver was sitting upright. My backup was my sergeant. He took one look at my pants, shook his head, and asked, 'Where's the head?' I shrugged.

"'Well, we got to find this kid's head,' the sergeant said.

"He gave me the job of retrieving the head. I walked down the road. It was littered with pieces of Ford convertible. The sudden stop and the shearing of the top had the effect of a catapult spewing pieces, including the victim's head, in all directions. Shit Creek was about twenty-five yards from the accident. You could smell it before you saw it. I got to the creek hoping I wouldn't have to go into it. With my nightstick, I began poking around. Even if I hit the head with my prodding, I wouldn't have known it. When was the last time you poked around in a creek for a decapitated head? Well, wouldn't you know, I did manage to disturb the waters enough for the head to bob up. I almost lost it again. Here was this head floating on the water looking right up at me. Jaw skin was rolled up like a window shade. Teeth were clinched. Eyes wide open. I called the sergeant."

"What did he do?" Milos asked.

"He strolled down to the creek with his snot rag covering his nose, paper shopping bag under his arm, and in one swipe grabbed the head by its hair and threw it into the bag. As he walked away, he mumbled, "Tough way to die. I hope St. John and Sons Funeral Home can do something with this.'"

Charlie went home that morning and found his wife on the couch fast asleep with the broken virgin statue held close to her heart. He kissed her gently on her forehead and lay down on the floor next to her.

Chapter 3
THE FIDDLE

Charlie's story of guts and gore was disturbing to the old timers. It was much later in their American experience that horrific, bloody scenes of slasher films would be commonplace on the movie screens. Real life came first, the motion picture depiction later.

Late Friday afternoon, during the holy season of Lent, about a week before Easter, a few of the regulars stopped by the store. The Sorrowful Mother Novena they were to attend started at seven p.m. It was five p.m. so they had a little time together before they made their way up Sophia Avenue to St. Benedict Church. The women of the parish throughout the year attended the novenas. Lent was a time of devotion, and the men of the parish would make a special effort to attend. The long workday would make it impossible for most men to attend. Novenas were scheduled for five, six, and seven p.m.

The novena of the Blessed Virgin Mary, or the Sorrowful Mother Novena, unlike a personal novena was a service led by the parish priest. The novena was colored by distinct Slovak tradition. The Slovak Ladies Sodality would arrive early to sing in Slovak before the service in the darkened church. The ladies, clothed in black with their babushkas, were led by one voice. The voice chanted a prayer that harked back one thousand years to the deep history of Catholic Slovakia. The rest joined in to fill the church with sorrowful heart-rendering notes. The service would be a mixture of prayers, litanies, and singing in English, Latin, and Slovak. At the beginning of the service the Eucharist would be on display in the monstrance. The ladies' sodality would sing the *Tanto Ergo* and the *Stabat Mater* a cappella. The service, lasting a half hour, would end in the benediction. The priest would leave the altar and the sodality would close the service with a Slovak prayer and the recitation of the holy rosary.

The hardware store closed at seven p.m. on weeknights. This night John closed early to accompany the men to novena. This was a special evening because John's brother, Nick, was in town. Stefan, the war veteran, Anton, the bowling alley owner, Milos the World War I veteran, and Joel, John's son, gathered at the back of the store. Joel put on a pot of coffee. Joel, in passing, blurted out that it would be great if he could learn to play the violin. After the group in unison chimed about the difficulty of learning the instrument, Nick approached Joel and said, "Sit down, boy, and stop squirming! So you want to play the fiddle?"

"Yeah, I mean yes, sir," Joel answered.

"First of all let me straighten you out on one little item; that is, a violin is referred to as a *fiddle* by practitioners of the instrument. They speak of their instrument as a fiddle."

"Yes, sir, fiddle."

"Good, see I got you started off in the right direction already! So when you are talking to a virtuoso, ah, like me, you speak of the instrument as a fiddle. Don't forget it!"

"Oh, I won't, sir."

Nick was not sure his nephew wouldn't forget it. Nick hadn't seen Joel and John in a few years. He would visit the hardware store when in town. Nick knew that the hardware business barely made enough money to support the Maders. Some said John didn't do so badly for his family of five boys; others knew he just got by. Nick knew that John just got by. Joel would grow up to be different from his four brothers. He would be the egghead of the family. He took after his older brother, Nicholas, Uncle Nick's namesake. Nicholas went to college to study business. Joel would go to college and study English.

This confused his grandma and grandpa, the immigrant Slovaks, who spoke very little English. Why would you go to college to study a language you knew perfectly well? It was a waste of money.

Joel was like his uncle Nick. Nick was an artist with paint, Joel with words. They both appreciated the fine arts. Nick realized early in life that artists couldn't make a living during the Depression, so he decided to go to Case Institute of Technology and study architectural design. Graduating with a college degree for a first-generation Slovak was unusual. Only three out of every hundred Slovaks would attain a college degree. He graduated and got a job with the federal government.

It wasn't long before he headed up a department of architects and was designing buildings of his own. His agency picked the two architectural firms that designed the Cleveland Federal Building. Years after the building's completion, he never missed a chance to visit it. Joel remembered that every Easter, uncle Nick would drive in from Chicago with his wife and children to visit his parents. He also managed to visit the federal building. He would take a cab by himself and go down to Ninth Street. He would never go into the building. He would just stand outside and look up. When he got tired of looking up, he would sit on a bench and talk to people who worked inside.

"How do you like the old bird?" he asked, pointing to the building. People weren't kind at times. Too modern, too straight up and down, too much glass, too many windows, too stark—on and on. He didn't mind. He learned long ago you couldn't please everyone. An artist pleases himself first. When it came to questions on the arts, he had plenty of advice and he gave it freely.

"Well now, you got yourself a pretty good program lined up here, if you are going to tackle the fiddle. Fiddle playing goes way back in our family history. Your grandfather's father played the fiddle at all the family weddings in the old country. The instrument and all its secrets were passed down from generation to generation. You will be one of many Maders who have tried his hand at this fiddle playing. Cherish that special feeling of picking up the fiddle and playing in the footsteps of your ancients. But as I was saying, I do manage to get a little fiddle playing in from time to time. I try a couple times a week to get at it. Ah, but you know, fiddle practicing is not too popular with people. I sort of enjoy it, but, you know what it is, it's the people around you that don't appreciate the same things that we do. Sit up, boy, don't slouch!"

"Oh, sorry, sir."

"That's better.

As I was saying, if you're going to practice this thing, you're going to have to do it in some kind of seclusion so you don't bother the people around you. Playing scales and the fingering exercises and the bowing and whatnot can irritate the hell out of people. It takes a couple of years before you are able to do very much with it. Did you know that every fiddle player sounds different? That's true. Listen to some old records of the greats and you will see what I mean. Same piece but different sound. Nevertheless, the fiddle is a very interesting instrument, and as difficult as it is, I think it still could offer a lot of pleasure and enjoyment to anybody who wants to take it up. Let's see, you're twelve years old?"

"Fourteen, sir."

"Well, that shouldn't be a deterrent because there are many people who took up a vocation or hobby late in life. After all, Grandma Moses started to paint when she was eighty, and she achieved a certain amount of fame and notoriety. Then there are others like this guy who peddles the Country Fried Chicken. He was broke at the age of sixty, and he made a fortune by the time he was sixty-five or seventy. He was a millionaire from nothing but fried chicken. So you see, there is still time for you and others like you to accomplish something with these little hobbies. Why, did you ever stop to think that you could be a doctor in eight years? I have heard young people play solos in a couple of years. I think it can be done!"

"I think so too!"

"You do?"

"Yes, sir."

"What are you doing for lessons?"

"I don't know. What do you suggest?"

"When I was taking lessons … let's see, how long ago was that? Taft was pres—no, Wilson was president. The war was still on. I was seven years old. I got this ten-dollar fiddle my mother bought me complete with a case and a bow and a piece of rosin and a First Violin Book. That was ten bucks. Back in those days you were able to get fiddle lessons for fifty cents an hour. I remember the old duffer who gave me the lessons. He was Hungarian. He seemed so old to me. I sure thought that the mere act of lifting a fiddle would kill 'im. He lived somewhere down there on Elwell off Woodhill Road. I recall trudging across Woodhill trying to hide from everybody I knew. I didn't want anyone to know I was carrying a fiddle. I'd get over there and we'd practice for about an hour. Damned near killed him to hear me play! I kept it up and began to play so people could make out the tune.

"Like I said, fiddle playing could be dangerous in the old neighborhood. There was this one time when I barely escaped with my life. I was two years into the fiddle when I attracted some unwanted attention on my way to my lesson. A group of boys hung out in front of Karkey's Delicatessen about a block from Elwell. The house where the lesson was given was about a half mile from home on Ambler Street. I would go up Sophia to Woodhill Road and head north to Elwell. This was way before your father had this hardware store. I think an A&P or a Kroger's was here. I would have to walk past Karkey's. Well, anyway, it didn't take much for the group of boys to see that I was carrying a musical instrument in my black case. The shape of the case was a dead giveaway. What followed was an episode of horror for me.

"'What you got in that black case, sissy boy?' Stash snarled. Stash was an eighth grader in Sister Veronica's class at St. Benedict's Elementary School. He was a big kid. His favorite activity was hanging around Karkey's delicatessen and tormenting younger kids.

"'Nothin',' I replied.

"'How can you say you have nothin'? No one carries nothin' in a case,' Larry retorted, bending over and whispering in my ear. Larry was about as big as Stash and was one grade behind him. His breath smelled like shit. Henry was the third boy in the gang. He was wiry and the most agile of the three. He gained his reputation by being in the ninth grade at Benedictine High School. He was the oldest and most experienced of the group. He looked down on us elementary school kids. Not a week would go by without Henry flattening one of us. I escaped his wrath by avoiding him. All three of the gang towered over me. On my own I had no chance of escape.

"There was one thing that I did have that would give me more strength then the three combined, and that was the fear of losing my violin. Your grandmother would have never forgiven me if I'd lost or broken the fiddle. She had to work hard cleaning houses for the Jewish ladies in the heights. Ten dollars was a months' pay for her. It was a standoff with the gang or sheer doom facing Grandma. The gang looked good in comparison.

"The crew was a hodgepodge of rags, patches, and suspenders. Their shirts and pants were shiny from food drippings and grease. Their shoes hardly resembled anything we would call a shoe today: theirs were layer upon layer of soles hastily attached by their fathers. They were sure to be handed down to a brother. They didn't wash much. They were lucky to get a bath once a week. Usually they shared the bath water with their brothers and sisters. The odor was most apparent by the end of the week during cold winter months. The janitor at the school would crank up the heat in the classrooms and the kids would percolate with the smells of stale, grimy unwashed underwear. Every liniment that was applied during the course of the week would add to the general funk. Hygiene classes were yet to be introduced in school.

"They were poor. They knew they were poor. Their clothes and empty stomachs proved it. Their fathers worked twelve-hour days in the steel mills. The pay was bad. The boys were lucky to see a piece of meat once a week. It was easy to avoid eating meat on Fridays. No hell for them because of that sin. The description fit all the children in the community, including me. I almost felt sorry for them—if it wasn't for them coming after my violin.

"Henry made a stab for the case. I ducked and turned and started to run back home. Larry, the smartest of the three, crossed Woodhill Road in traffic and headed toward Sophia Avenue about a block away. He knew where I lived and was going to go down Woodhill Court, an alley running perpendicular to Woodhill Road, and down to Ambler. He had in mind to cut me off at Sophia and Ambler. Stash and Henry were hard on my behind. I was small but fast. I kept ahead of them. I had incentive: the violin.

"I got to Sophia and looked down the street and saw Larry. I knew I couldn't go that way. So I kept running past Tatra Bank, Petras Bakery and Seiman Hardware, the Hungarian hardware store, till I got to the library on the corner of Parkview. I thought for a minute to run into the library but thought better of it. Librarians could be very nice to adults but it was a different story with kids. Besides, the uglies would just wait for me until I came out.

"I thought the only chance I had was to make a break for it across the street and down to the field. The field was between Mt. Auburn and Manor. Right where Woodhill Road turned into Ninety-Third Street. It was on the opposite side of the street of the CTS Car Barns. If I made the field I knew I could lose them. The field was actually a hill overgrown with weeds leading down to a railroad siding. I made my break. I ran across the cinder parking lot and made my way to the road leading down the embankment. I got as far as Shit Creek when I noticed Henry was already there, about fifty yards to the right of me. Larry was right behind me. Stash was up on the railroad tracks on the other side of the foul pool. I was trapped. They knew I was trapped. They must have cut through Ninety-Second Street and then behind Ohio Forge. Their faces, all grimy and sweaty, had that look of satisfaction of outwitting their prey. I felt sick. I knew what would come next.

"Larry grabbed me, took my precious violin, laid it on the ground, and threw me into Shit Creek pool. I couldn't swim but managed to hold on to some branches of a dead tree that lay partially beneath the surface of the brown ugly waters.

"By this time Henry and Stash opened the violin case and began playing tug-o-war with my fiddle. Larry grabbed the bow and began hitting my head with it. Stash wrenched the violin from Henry and threw it on the ground and began to kick it to pieces.

"Larry, pleased with what Henry did, began taunting me again. 'See, you little shit? You shouldn't have run away. You are shit and you smell like shit too!' Flinging what was left of my fiddle high into the air, it fell back to Earth, hitting me square in the head. I went down underwater, gulped an unhealthy mouthful of putrid water, and resurfaced to see the three walking away shouting, alternating in Hungarian and English, 'The little shit now smells like shit.'

"I managed to pull myself out of the water. I lay on the side of the abyss puking my guts out. The sour-egg smell, the metallic taste followed me around for the rest of my life. Even to this day, some fifty years later, I can still smell that ugly, rancid, rotten-egg-like odor. I was able to fish what was left of my fiddle out of the pool. I held it in my hands and pulled it close to my chest. Here was something I loved, broken beyond anyone's ability to fix. Here was the present my mother had worked a whole month on her knees scrubbing floors to earn the money to buy. Here was my instrument, my buddy, who kept me company for the last two years. Here, hanging in the air above the fiddle, was the last work I had mastered on its strings: the theme from the overture from the opera *Raymond*. That music and my fiddle were gone. Here I held what signified a tradition that went back hundreds of years in my family, smashed and lost forever.

"I no longer cared what would happen to me. My mother's wrath could not be equal to my own sorrow. I started up the hill, fiddle and case in hand, reeking from the Shit Creek smell. I felt tired, defeated, and alone. My head hurt. The muscles of my legs turned into mush. I wasn't in any mood to go home.

"No one would miss me for another hour or two, so I decided to work my way across Woodhill Road to the CTS Car Barn's administration building where there was a public bathroom. All noses were on me as I walked through the main entrance. One of the trolley drivers told me to get the hell out of there because I stank like shit. I quickly ran out into the yard full of trolleys. It was already late and most of the rush was over so the yard was full. A small kid my size could easily lose himself amongst these modern marvels of transportation. I went about six rows in and about ten trolleys up the line. I found trolley 33 with its doors partially opened and forced myself in. I was able to pull the remnants of my fiddle through with me. I walked down the narrow aisle all the way to the back of the trolley. I carefully place the fiddle next to me on a seat next to the rear entrance of the trolley. I laid down and immediately fell asleep.

"I wasn't missed until about four hours later. Back then a missing boy was no big problem. Parents usually assumed he was off at the playground with friends. But Mother and Dad knew I wasn't the playground type. They both got scared and decided to ask around. Karkey was the only one who could remember seeing me that day. A quick check with the violin teacher revealed I had never made the lesson. No one else could be found to help. This was a time when you didn't run to the police. Friends formed groups of two or three and went about the neighborhood looking for this little lost fiddle player. I, in somnolent bliss, knew nothing of the commotion stirring around me.

The routine of the car barns was the cleaning crew would come in about six p.m. and begin systematically sweeping out each trolley. A cleaner named Marge opened up trolley 33 and was immediately taken aback by the smell. She called a supervisor, and they both came into the car and found shitty me. The searchers were notified, and I was returned to mother and father, smell and all.

"Your grandmother took one look, smelled me and the fiddle and the case, and groaned. Your grandfather said in Slovak, 'Lena, don't be hard on him. He seems barely alive.'

That evening he told them the whole story of what had happened to me. Surprisingly, they didn't punish me. Mother just held me as father washed me with lye soap in our porcelain claw-foot bathtub. Into bed I went with hugs, kisses, and prayers of gratitude.

"That night, Mother asked Father what they were to do about the boys who had beaten me up and broke my fiddle. Father whispered, 'We will buy the boy another violin and do nothing about the boys.'

"Henry, Stash, and Larry were never held responsible for what happened.

"Henry's father was my father's boss and responsible for the weekly payroll.

Besides, he was Hungarian."

Chapter 4
HIS BAG

The men went to novena that evening. Joel made up his mind to learn to play the violin and continue the tradition. The tale was of a time long ago. Stefan, the only Hungarian of the group, took no offense at the underlining meaning of the story: Hungarians were not much liked. Moreover, the tale showed once again that Slovaks were never troublemakers. Because of their unskilled status and previous lack of opportunity, Slovaks, by their nature, were submissive. Their work ethic made them valuable. Their submissiveness made them targets of exploitation. By the time the "fiddle" story was retold in the hardware store some thirty years after the action, ethnic lines were blurred enough so that all were accepted. After all, didn't John Mader marry Mary Sedlak? Mary's father was Hungarian.

Sometime later, during one of those glorious spring days in Cleveland, a day that even Chaucer would be envious of, Stefan came crashing through the back door of the hardware store and landed in the middle of the lunch group. He was fuming about the doctors at the state mental hospital. His brother, Alex, was a patient at "Turney Tech," as it was called. Stefan was so upset that he reverted to speaking in Hungarian. His tirade was punctuated by calling the wrath of all the Hungarian saints on his oppressors, the staff of the hospital. Stefan never had anything good to say about the hospital staff. His friends did not want to hear about another episode of the hospital. They could recite, like a litany, the perceived injustices of the doctors, nurses, and staff of the "hospital." The group managed to settle him down and to distract him; they asked him what he had in his bag.

"The bag—everyone worries about what is in my bag," Stefan shot back. Henrich, the Pratt and Lambert salesman, a German, garbled in Hungarian, "Forget about it. Just cool down!" Forget about it Steve would not. He was on a roll and felt pushed to tell his story of his bag.

In perfect Hungarian he would tell his story.

"It was February. The snow was pretty high. I was going to Kroger's then, and of course the new Pick-n-Pay wasn't around. They had Fishers on upper Buckeye Road and—"

"Yeah," Milos interrupted, "I remember when it used to be there. It was an old-time store just like the old butcher shop I used to work in."

"This must be back," he continued, "about, I would say—let me see, it's gonna be four years that my brother David died—could be six years ago. I carried a bag then too, you see, but it wasn't a green one; it was a blue one, and I wore it out."

"Yeah, I remember, I remember, you wear out a bag a year," Pavol, the plumbing salesman, said.

Stefan was a veteran of WWII. He'd served as a medic in the South Pacific. Joel recalled all the times he would stop in his father's hardware store on Woodhill Road and chew the fat. He recalled the war stories Stefan told. He recalled his father and Stefan had a love-hate relationship. Joel remembered, depending on Stefan's mood, his father would love or hate him. He recalled that Stefan was odd. He never cussed. If someone were telling a dirty joke, he would walk away. Joel remembered that he was Catholic. That was good. He knew he was Hungarian. That was bad.

Yes, Stefan always carried a bag. What was in his bag was his business and no one else's. No matter how interesting the subject, Stefan never lost sight of his tightly closed, colored bag.

Stefan went on. "So my sister says, 'Here's five dollars: get Hawaiian Punch, get this grapefruit juice, get a carton of Kools king size.' I says okay She told me that in the night, so the next day I went to Kroger's." Stefan stopped, put his bag carefully down on the floor next to the heater grate in the floor, pulled a pinch of snuff out of a tin, sucked it into his nose, and continued.

"I walked inside Kroger's. I never paid attention to nobody. I am walkin' around. I can't find the grapefruit juice, but in the meantime I got the Kools king size. I walked all the way around and everything. I got the four cans of Hawaiian Punch, but I can't find the grapefruit juice! I'm lookin' around and around with my bag in one hand and Hawaiian Punch and cigarettes in the other. I can't see good. When I look at somethin', tilting not only my eyes but my whole head down, my eyes go down in such a direction that it's like a magnifying glass. I can see better.

"Then I see a blonde girl. You know the type. At work, but all made up like she was going to go out on a date that minute. I always saw her inside there. I don't know what she was. Later on I found out that she was the assistant manager. The manager wasn't there. They had this small, little blonde girl in his place.

"So I'm walkin' around lookin' at this, lookin' at that. I see this girl watching me makin' off she's workin', you know, watchin' me. I don't pay attention. I thought maybe it's my imagination. I go around the corner. She goes down on the other end and swings through the center aisle."

"She's following you," Henrich said.

"Yeah," Stefan answered, "she's following me. I says, 'You son of a gun, you think I'm a crook!' So, I take my good old time lookin' at everything because I'm gonna hold her there and waste her time. I got lots of time, don't you know. I know she's watchin' me now. I'm stallin'. I'm going from one aisle to the other aisle. Up this aisle down the next. She's watchin' me and I sees that she's watchin' me.

"I came to the garden seed rack. February, you know, and so they're selling seeds already! I went over there and was lookin' at *all* the seeds. I don't care a darn about seeds. I don't care nothin' about seeds. I'm just stallin'. You know. Then I got mad and turned around and yelled clear across the store, 'What are you followin' me for?'"

"What did she say?"

"She says all snotty, 'You know you shouldn't be walking around the store with a bag.' I says to her there's nothin' around here that tells me that I can't come in here with a bag. Furthermore, when I come to a store, I want to shop. I don't want to read no bulletin board with a bunch of lousy rules on it. You have nothin' over here to show me that I'm not allowed to shop with my own bag.

"By this time she is really mad. You can tell because this wart on her chin becomes a bright red and her cakey, made-up skin got all blotchy. She yells back at me. 'Take a cart!' I says, 'I don't want to push a cart. I'm not buying that much.' Then I yelled, 'Who's the manager around here!' You should have seen her. She turned and walked away. In retreat, she glanced over her shoulder and scowled with her warty face. I won this time.

"I finally found the grapefruit juice. So I carried the bag to the checkout counter, and the line was real long. I was between the shelves and women were comin' for things and they would say, 'May I step through please?' So I says okay. I was lookin' at things as I was going down. Finally I came to this cash register place. I was about two away. It looked to me like the assistant manager came and says to this colored fella that was packin' groceries, a kid about eighteen, 'Did you go to dinner yet?' Whether this was a code for them I don't know. But this register girl was talky. She's Italian. She's got a scabby growth right here on her forehead. She's got more diamonds on her ring than I don't know what. They'll blind you when you get close to her.

"So I'm waitin' and waitin'. Then the woman packs up her stuff in front of me. Then I'm next! I put the Hawaiian Punch, grapefruit juice and Kools king size right next to her stuff, and I am holdin' my bag. All I was thinkin' about was how I could get through this line and out. I already had the five dollars out. It was a beat up five-dollar bill. Finally, I came to her, the cash register girl. I said these are the only things I have. She looked at me, and she cashed the five dollars out and gave me the change.

"So before I got to the end of the counter to walk around, the colored kid stopped me. I says, 'You needn't put it in a bag. There is room in my bag for all these things. I got my own bag.' The colored kid already had a big Kroger bag. You know the large one that holds about twenty dollars' worth of junk. Then he says to me, he says, 'Dump your things in here.' I says, 'I only bought this. I haven't got nothin'. I don't need a big bag like that.'

"What do you mean?" I asked, "Did he want you to dump all your things from your bag into his Kroger bag?"

"Yeah. He said, 'Dump everything in here.' I refused. The girl came out from the cash register and blocked me with her hand. She cut me off. She says to me, 'You know we have a right to inspect that bag.' I says that's true. She says, 'Well, we want to know what you got in the bag. Dump it on to the counter.' I says, 'I am not dumpin' nothin' nowhere.' She says, 'But we have a right to look at it.' I says you have a right to look at it if you call the Cleveland Police here. Then I will dump it on the counter when they tell me to. I'm dumpin' nothin' nowhere.' By this time a crowd of people had gathered because I was shoutin', 'Don't you see?' So the cash register girl, seeing that I'm stubborn, says, 'Oh, all right you can go!' I asked, 'Are you sure everything is all right?' She says, 'Yes you can go!' I asked again, 'Are you sure?' She yelled, 'Yes!' and then I says, 'In that case I will let you and this group of ladies see what I have in this blue bag.' I turned it over and dumped all my underwear, dirty shorts and all, out onto the counter and spread them out nicely.

"The colored kid said, 'Oh, shit!' I said, 'Yes, a little on the underwear, but I am going to the laundromat to wash them.'

Chapter 5
THE BOXCAR

Jozef Mader was John's father. He would help at the hardware store. He did the odd jobs around the place. He swept the floor, filled glass gallon jugs with turpentine, paint thinner and linseed oil, and helped make porch paint by mixing paint cans of mixed sizes into a large fifty-five-gallon barrel. Later he would ladle out one gallon at a time of Mader's special gray porch paint. All colors of paint went into the batch except red. Red would never break down into gray, the desired color. He would knead the stiff putty from large cans and put it into small cans. John learned the retail game early on: buy by the pound and sell by the ounce.

Jozef was not a large man. In his youth, he was five feet, eight inches, weighed two hundred pounds. His hair was prematurely gray—not really gray but silver, almost white. His face had the look of a central European, round and ruddy. He prided himself in being clean-shaved every day. The rest of his body was made tough by the years of laying brick for the city. His longest-held job was working on a street crew in Cleveland. The streets were all made of small red bricks. The bricks weighed about five pounds each. In his lifetime, he carefully placed thousands of bricks side by side, yard after yard, and eventually mile after mile. Clothes were the least of his worries. His daily wardrobe was the same flannel red shirt and gray cotton pants. Shoes were high tops and black. When he entered the room, everyone gave him a respectful greeting. He was the old timer. Jozef was the one who started it all here in America for the Maders. The year was 1956.

John gave Jozef a special job this day. He was to try to find a missing plumber's wrench recently absent from the workbench in the back of the store. He looked everywhere in the store. No wrench. Even before he started to look for the wrench, he suspected that the wrench was not in the store. Jozef knew John's tools were there for the borrowing. Unlike tool rental stores of years to come, customers did not have to leave credit card deposits. They just went into the back of the hardware store and took the tool that was needed for the job at home. The customer yelled out, "Hey, John, I need to take a pipe wrench. I'll bring it back tomorrow." Not every borrower would remember to bring the tool back "tomorrow." John never remembered who took what.

The usual suspects would be the guys who came to the store for lunch and a chat. Jozef would ask each one, "When are you going to return John's red Rigid wrench?" The individuals would smile to hear "Stod," the old one, say the alliterative line "red Rigid wrench" in broken English. One after another, they would deny borrowing the wrench. When the wrench seemed lost forever, one of the crew would suddenly confess he had it. "I forgot all about it. It's in the trunk of my car. I'll go get it."

Anton, the owner of a small construction company, brought the wrench back with a report that a body had been found under Woodhill Road Bridge by Buckeye Road right down the street from his office. "The police think it was a suicide," he said. "Jumped in front of a rapid transit car. The body was cut in half. No head either. They are still looking for the head as I speak."

Jozef shuttered when he heard this news. It reminded him of an incident that had occurred twenty years ago—an incident he had tried to forget. His uneasiness did not go unobserved. One of the men asked Stod what was bothering him. What he told them would forever change the way they thought of their neighborhood.

Jozef heard about it from his friends who worked on the railroad. They were talking about it in church on Sunday. It was July 1936, during the height of the Great Depression. The boxcar was on a siding on Eighty-Seventh Street near Kinsman Road, not far down from the field, where in years to come his grandchildren would play. It was there for the taking. All he had to do was break it apart and carry it up Manor Avenue hill. Manor ran perpendicular to Woodhill Road. That was the hard part: carrying the wood up the hill. Building materials were expensive, and Jozef needed to build a garage in the back of his house. Everyone on the street had a garage. He didn't want to be different. After living on Manor for a while, Jozef soon learned why they called it Woodhill. Every walk seemed uphill. Jozef could carry the lumber up the hill. He had the time. But what really bothered him most was how he would explain to anyone, like a policeman, what he was doing. He didn't have the words. Although he he'd been in this country for twenty-three years, he'd never learned the language beyond the basics. He was thirty years old when he came to Cleveland. He was now fifty-three. This was way past the time of easy language acquisition. Sure he understood most of what was said to him. He just wasn't sure of himself. Besides, everyone of importance in his life spoke Slovak and lived close by in the neighborhood. It was times like this that he wished he were back in the old country.

The old country was Slovakia. He was born on a farm on the steppes of the Carpathian Mountains by the Danube and Moravia rivers, not far from the capital, Bratislava. Jozef and his brothers owned this fertile land. When he was born in 1883, the farm was already in his father's hands. When his father died, the farm passed down to his sons. This was no small accomplishment. Slovakia was a part of the great Austria-Hungarian Empire and property rights were always questionable. Franz Joseph was the emperor. There was no Slovak state or government in the nineteenth century. There wasn't a period of time that Slovakia and Hungary weren't at each other's throats. Hungary dominated Slovakia. The Hungarians always felt superior to the Slovaks. In the schools, the Slovak children would be forced to learn the Magyar language. The parish priests would have to preach their sermons in Hungarian. The greatest insult would be the changing of Slovak names to Hungarian names. Jozef Mader became Joszef Magyar. The Slovaks hated the Hungarians. They were overseers. They were the ones who kept their country in bondage. Even their language was different. Its stem traced to no Slavic roots. "They were nothing but a bunch of oriental hillbillies," Jozef whispered.

Jozef spat on the ground. *Hungarians,* he thought. But that was all in the past. The farm and his brothers were just a memory. Even the reason he'd gotten mad at his brothers and left the old country was a bit of a blur. He remembered it vaguely, something about being lazy and not doing enough around the farm. His job was to take care of the cows and butcher the pigs. He would get up at five in the morning, walk out to the barn, and milk the cows and slop the pigs. He remembered how cold it was in the winter and how in order to keep warm he would take off his shoes and step in the warm cow manure. He remembered that he felt he was better than just being a tender of cows. So he left. Now he was in America. He wanted to be an American. He wanted to fit in with the others in America.

Jozef came to this country in 1913. He brought his family of wife, Magdalena, and two sons Joseph and Nicholas. His youngest son, John, was born that same year on a small nondescript street off Woodhill Road called Ambler. This was a commitment to the future. Unlike other Slovak immigrants of the great Slavic immigration to America, he planned to stay. Most Slovak immigrants came with the idea of staying in America for a year to earn enough money to return to Slovakia and live a little easier. After all, it was known in every village in Slovakia that the streets of America were paved with gold. Grab a brick or two, head home, and live like the emperor. No, Jozef and his family were here to stay. Jozef heard there was a Slovak community in Cleveland, and in that community was St. Ladislas Church. This was the first church for Slovak Catholics in Cleveland. He learned about it when he was "processed" at Ellis Island. The parish priest at St. Ladislas in Cleveland, Ohio, would be the one to talk to for help in getting started in the land of the free.

The little family nestled in a small apartment on Ambler Avenue just west of Woodhill Road. The lodging was a room attached to the back of the owner's home. No kitchen, no bathroom, and room enough for one bed. Jozef thought even these accommodations were better than the mud floor home of the old country. What disturbed the family most was the landlord was Hungarian. They didn't much like Hungarians. Jozef and Lena spoke fluent Hungarian. They had to in order to survive in the old country. Their new "Slovak" church's congregation was evenly divided between Slovaks and Hungarians. Eventually the church split, and the Hungarians built their own church, St. Elizabeth's on Buckeye Road. Estvan, the Hungarian landlord, was a devout Roman Catholic and that was the only thing good.

Magdalena, "Lena," Jozef's wife, was ready for a change after eleven long years of sharing a bathroom and kitchen with Estvan's family. She gathered her savings of $1540 for a down payment and went off and bought a three-family house at 9600 Manor. Lena was a strong-willed woman who was in charge of the family. Three sons made it impossible to live on Ambler. So she bought, without consulting Jozef, the Manor home.

Jozef and Magdalena were married in Devinska Nova Ves, a small town in the old country, in 1908. Jozef knew Lena was the one for him when he saw her tending the pigs in her back yard. He thought if she was good enough to tend to the pigs, she surely could look after him. They never dreamed that their life together would last sixty-five years and end across the Atlantic Ocean hundreds of miles away in Cleveland, Ohio.

Pigs, cows, chickens, and vegetables were their life. Jozef's farm was whole and was located alongside the Small Carpathian Mountains. He was lucky. Unlike some of the Slovak farmers whose land was spread out over distant tracts, his land was next to his house. The farmers of Slovakia followed the fertile land. Because of the disjointed nature of the terrain, some Slovak farmers suffered. All the tools of their labor had to be lugged a distance before actual work could take place. Before tending to the fields, the cows had to be milked and the pigs slopped. Jozef became very good at the slaughter. Meat was very scarce. All the farm could support were six cows and five pigs and a few chickens. The pigs made the holy day feasts. Pigs were slaughtered before Christmas and Easter. Jozef would do the whole job in an hour. He could kill, bleed, gut, skin, and quarter the animal in an hour. He would cut the hams with the precision of a surgeon. He was so fast and precise that other farmers would call on him to butcher their pigs. Jozef was very proud of this. He liked to show off his skill to Lena and her father. He kept his knives sharp and always ready. His reward for helping others was the pig's feet. Pickled pig's feet were a delicacy.

Jozef's knives would come with him to America. He thought everyone in America had pigs just like in Slovakia. Where there were pigs, there always would be a need for a butcher.

Jozef laughed thinking back now after living in America for so many years. He thought the stupid Clevelanders didn't even know where hams came from. Everything was processed and wrapped neat and pretty. No show of blood of the slaughter for the Americans! Outside of a few chickens he slaughtered in his basement from time to time on Manor, that part of his life was over.

Now the problem was to get the wood from the boxcar up Manor hill and into his backyard. Before he began dismantling the boxcar, he dug a shallow foundation for the garage. He mixed and poured all the cement by hand. When that was done, he decided to take a first look at the boxcar. It was late, so he thought tomorrow would be soon enough to get started.

The sun toyed with Stod as he lay in bed looking out the bedroom window at the apple tree he had just planted this last week. The apples would be green and sour. He didn't know this at the time. He just knew it was an apple tree. He would soon learn that the tree would bear fruit that would make Lena happy. He didn't know that by the time Lena died in 1972, she would have made more than a thousand apple pies and hundreds of quarts of applesauce from the fruit of this small sprig. The tree was presently far from bearing that harvest. The first apple bounty would be at least two years away. Thirty-eight years later the apple tree would be dead. So would Stod.

It was the work of the sun on the apple tree that woke him this morning. The apple tree cast the smallest spidery shadow on the bedroom wall, enough to make the room look different, enough to make him question if he was in his own home. He looked over at Lena to assure himself that all was right. He got up ever so slowly. It was Saturday, and Lena worked hard all week. Tomorrow was the day to rise early for church. Today she should rest. If he could only get out of bed without waking her. He looked up and saw the crucifix on the wall across from their bed. He bowed his head and whispered, "All for the honor and glory of Jesus Christ." He inched his way into the kitchen and put on a pot of coffee. Jozef looked into the front room that doubled as a living room during the day and a bedroom for John at night. John was fast asleep on the couch.

The Manor house had three suites. Jozef and Lena's suite consisted of three rooms and a bath. The three rooms were attached to the back of the house. The two front suites were identical four rooms and a bathroom one on top of the other. When Jozef and Magdalena first moved into the house, they lived in the front rooms downstairs. The house had a large basement that over time would be a place where parties were held; model train layouts would be set up; chickens would be slaughtered; wine and soap would be made; and the family wash would be done.

Lena's oldest son, Joseph, and his wife, Sally, occupied the upstairs suite. The downstairs rooms were rented. The extra money was what allowed Lena to pay off the mortgage early and live without assistance during the long Depression. Jozef's middle son, Nicholas, was in Chicago working for the government.

Stod wrote a note to Lena saying not to worry; he was going down the street to have a look at the boxcar that was soon to be his new garage. The kitchen door opened into a common hallway with the front rooms. Stod stood in the hallway for a minute to listen for any sounds. All was quiet. He made his way down to the basement to retrieve a wooden toolbox. He prepared the toolbox the night before. He made sure he had the basic tools for the dismantling job. The box held a crowbar, a claw hammer, a screwdriver, a pair of pliers, a handsaw, and one small boning knife for cutting the bit of sausage, cheese, and bread Lena made for his lunch.

The hallway door to the outside driveway sat about three quarters of the way back from the front of the house. Stod carefully opened the door and put his hand on the outer copper mesh, wire-clothed, wooden screen door. The morning edition of the *Cleveland Plain*

Dealer was nestled between the two doors. The front downstairs tenant's paper. He picked it up and glanced at the headline and recognized only one word of the large bold headline: "Butcher." It was one of the few English words his son, John, had taught him. The rest of the headline was meaningless. He placed the paper on the landing next to the renter's door. Carefully closing the door, not to wake anyone, Stod stepped into the driveway alongside the house. The red brick driveway separated the neighbor's house from Stod's house by about fifteen feet—five feet of grass included. It had rained the night before and Jozef saw small little puddles formed where the driveway bricks sank into their sand base. He knew his next job would be to repair the driveway after he retrieved the wood from the boxcar and built the garage.

His house faced north. He walked about forty feet to the front of the house and looked up and down the street. Down the street was to the northwest and to the railroad spur on 87th Street. The street consisted of thirty-four houses between 93rd Street to 97th Street. There were many more houses "up the street" between 97th and 102nd and continuing to East Boulevard where Manor ended. Twenty-five houses stood on Stod's side of the street and nine houses on the other side. Each house had a small patch of grass that was the front yard. The sidewalks were made of gray sandstone, and at intervals a large

"W" was chiseled into them to indicate that a water shutoff was nearby. Cross the street a third of the way down and the row of houses suddenly stopped and the fence of the car barn began.

The Cleveland Electric Railway yard, the car barn, on Woodhill Road was sandwiched between Mt. Auburn on its north and Manor on its south side. At the front door of its administration building, the southern terminus of Woodhill Road began. A seven-foot high green wooden fence surrounded the whole yard. The boards of the structure were two-by-eight-inches wide secured by nails; they became unhinged as the nails rusted. The neighborhood kids would work the boards loose at the bottom and crawl under the fence to play among the streetcars.

Stod walked down the street with his toolbox in a wooden wheelbarrow. The wheelbarrow had been an afterthought. Stod made the wheelbarrow out of scrap wood. It was large like the ones he remembered from the old country: the kind that could transport half a household. It was so large that the toolbox all but vanished at its bottom. Although it was heavy to wheel, he was very strong and the barrow would make the job easier.

As he passed each house, he named the owners: the Chorbas and Ondas lived next door. Then came the Baileys and Fraziers two and three doors down. The Balogs and Vinciks and Haydens were further down the street. Stod's part of the street ended with Kupcik's Grill on the corner of Ninety-Third across from the car barns southern portal. Later in the history of this trolley yard a maintenance building would be erected within the confines of the fence. The air hammers used to remove the lugs of the tires of the trackless trolleys disturbed the peace of the street. No one complained about the noise. Noise meant that men had jobs and could feed their families.

When he got to the end of the street in front of Kupcik's Grill, he was tempted to stop and have a drink with some of his countrymen who just got off from work. He looked into the opened door to see if he recognized any of his friends but turned quickly. He said no to that urge and consoled himself by saying later at the end of the day's work would be soon enough. He thought, *Lena would be proud of me for resisting the temptation.* He crossed Ninety-Third Street and headed down the part of Manor that turned into a hill. The street dead-ended at Eighty-Seventh Street by a railroad siding. A rail track turnout led into a spur where the boxcar was located. He looked up the siding and caught his first glance of the old boxcar and the work that was ahead of him.

Something didn't feel right. Urban warning signs were flashing in his head. You know those unaccounted feelings and mental warnings that sound that remind a person that the rules of city life are different from the country. Stod was a country boy, but he learned the city rules quickly: don't stare at anyone too long; say excuse me when you accidentally bump someone on the trolley; and don't interfere when strangers are arguing. "Maybe this is not such a good idea after all. I have no right to be here. This is not my land. This is not my property. The boxcar belongs to someone. I will turn back," Stod whispered. That was his Catholic conscience at work—overtime. Did he really think he could take something that was not his? The boxcar was there for the taking. Or was it? Were his friends right about this? The thought of having his own garage didn't seem that important anymore. Taking something that didn't belong to him would earn him a place in hell. Turning to go back to the street but hesitating, he thought, *But what could it hurt to take a look?* He would not go to hell for just taking a look. *Why not take one little peek?* His church friends could be right.

Just as he turned again to go down the siding, the urban signs were replaced by another feeling. Something was wrong here. It was as if a thousand eyes were focused on this unassuming man. Stod quickly turned and froze, searching, peering into the brush that lined either side of the railroad tracks. Was someone watching him? No one there. *Forget it,* he thought. A sound. Stod turned again, faced the street, and saw the tail end of a car moving slowly down the road.

Enough already, he thought, *stop this right now. You came all this way to get some wood for the garage, and you are going to do it. There is no one watching. No one cares if you dismantle that old, rotting boxcar. Get to work and shut up already."*

Someone was watching Stod.

The boxcar presented itself. Unlike pictures that skew perspective, this workhorse of the last half of the nineteenth century was huge. Stod got up close and was taken aback by its size. He would live long enough to experience fifty foot, steel-frame, roller-bearing, and cast-steel examples of boxcars that would dwarf this car. How was he ever going to take this thing apart? One piece at a time of course. It was old, weathered, and rotting. Some of the boards were unsalvageable.

Stod thought, *Too far gone. Still, there is enough to build a modest garage.* The car was thirty-six feet long by eight feet high, the standard for vintage nineteenth-century boxcars. Its trucks were massive and raised the car high off the tracks. It had a faded red exterior boxcar. The red was a tinner's red, the same color red that builders used to paint the insides of gutters on nineteenth- and early twentieth-century houses. The vertical sideboards showed holes and white bleached weathered spots that obscured the boxcar's markings.

Jozef climbed the iron ladder that was on the car's side to look at the roof. He immediately realized that was a mistake. The first step, the one that hung from the floor frame of the boxcar, gave way to Jozef's weight. Stod found himself on the ground looking up. His first thought was whether he broke something. A quick inventory of his body parts revealed he was all right. The second thought was to go slow and check out everything before he acted.

He managed to get up the ladder and check out the roof. No solid wood there. That simplified things, just use the sides. He came down from the roof and inspected the sliding door located in the middle of the car. He thought if he couldn't get the door opened, his work here would be done. His only real chance at removing the boards would be from the inside of the car. The boxcar sat too high up off the tracks because of its huge trucks making it impossible for him to strip the wood from outside the car. He would need at least a twelve-foot ladder. He'd barely gotten the wheelbarrow and toolbox down the hill. A ladder would be out of the question.

The door opened easily, a testament to nineteenth-century railroad craftsmen. These cars, with proper maintenance, were built to last. Jozef hoisted himself up, belly first, hobo-style, into the boxcar. The inside of the car was dark and dank and smelled of urine. At one side of the car was a torn, muddy blanket lying against the wall. Next to the blanket were opened tin food cans. He picked one up and tossed it. Rancid. Someone had made this his home. Stod inspected the blanket. Stod realized what he had first thought was mud was blood. The cloth smelled. It was an odor he knew. Dry blood. A lot of dry blood.

Stod thought, *If this is human blood, the person is dead.* There was no other clothing. Just the blanket. *Someone lived and maybe died here*

Just go home. Stod's inner voice started again. He stopped the thought. No, he was going to continue with what he came to do.

He jumped out of the car and pulled the wheelbarrow closer to his work. He carefully hoisted his toolbox to the floor of the car. He left his lunch in the barrow and climbed back next to the tools. He reached into the toolbox for his claw hammer and crow bar. It was nine a.m. and the sun was hot. Stod learned early on that summers in Cleveland could be brutal. Three hours of hard work would bring him to noon, prayers, and lunch. That would be enough for one day. He would stop at noon, eat lunch, and take his treasure up the hill home. It would take him at least an hour to haul the wood home. Maybe he would even stop for a beer at Kupcik's.

To Jozef's relief, the sidewalls came down easily. The nails, bolts, and screws that held the boards and hardware together were well rusted and broke under pressure. In some places the boards could be pulled loose by hand.

He was making good progress when he heard the church bells ringing for the angelus. It was noon. Here in America as it was done in Slovakia this devout immigrant stopped to say the angelus.

Stod began, "The Angel of the Lord declared unto Mary: and she conceived of the Holy Spirit."

It took Jozef all of two minutes to recite the prayer. Some less devout could muddle through it without thinking of the profound mystery of the words. Jozef was not one of those Catholics. He meditated on this mystery of the incarnation. He was a primitive Christian. He never stopped marveling at the belief that God sent his Son down to Earth to save him and his family. "All for the honor and glory of Jesus Christ," Stod whispered.

Stod opened his lunch bag and pulled out his small butcher knife and began cutting up the sausage and Swiss cheese Lena had packed for him. His knife made quick work of the meal. When he held this knife, old feelings rushed over his being. He remembered the old country, his brothers, and his pigs. He was homesick. It was a long time since he left Devenska. He thought he was over these feelings. He knew he was not. This tool, this knife gave him comfort. It was a part of his tradition and of a time long ago.

Lunch was finished. He was cleaning his knife when his mind's voice alerted him. Someone was watching him. This time it was closer to him. Knife in hand, he turned quickly to confront whoever or whatever it was that took an interest in his doings. Nothing. No, something. There over in the brush about fifty yards down the track. Someone. Yes, and that someone was coming toward him. Stod measured the man; he was a big man. He was too far away to add any more to the description. With the sunlight behind the stranger, all Stod saw was a blotted dark figure. Jozef slowly lowered his knife. He didn't want the stranger to be frightened. He could use some company. Maybe it is one of his railroad friends? Maybe they could go and have a beer?

Just as he raised his hand to greet the stranger and wave him on, another wanderer came out of the brush right next to him. "What you doin', old timer?" the new stranger asked.

Stod understood the "what you doing" words, but "old timer" didn't register. "I bust 'em up. Make garage."

The new stranger didn't see the first man. Stod looked over the stranger's shoulder. The other man vanished.

Stod, distracted by the questions, forgot about the dark figure down the tracks.

"*Lump*," Slovak for "bum," Stod said under his breath.

This "lump" looked as if he was a neighbor but never a close friend of a straight razor. His black hair, set back behind a large forehead, took on a life of its own. Flies and yellow jackets dive-bombed the waxy strings. An occasional swat was his only acknowledgement of this flying circus. The gray, once-white shirt hung loosely on his shoulders. All the smells and leavings of vittles of the last hundred miles of rail riding could be traced splotch by splotch on his front and sleeves. Over his left arm hung a suit coat that bore no resemblance to his pants. His brimmed, creased, domed, dirty hat dangled from his free hand. He held a vegetable basket full of stuff of the road in his other hand. His pants, belted, holey, baggy, and too big took on the look of a vaudevillian comic. His shoes were never in danger of being stolen.

One feature did stand out—his eyes. They seemed to open Stod up like a surgeon's knife. As Jozef was looking at the stranger, the man seemed to be dissecting the whole scene. He slowly glanced around at the boxcar. Saw the car's door was opened. Saw the dirty blanket. He spotted the wheelbarrow, the leftover lunch, the small butcher knife in Stod's hand. He looked up and down the siding.

Stod's level of anxiety raised when the wanderer's returned glance settled on him. He was not just looking at Stod. He was inventorying him, much in the same way a doctor would examine a new patient. Whatever misgivings Jozef had about this day's adventure were now amplified and came crashing down on him. He became visibly shaken.

The stranger apparently picked up on this and asked, "What's a matter, old man? You never seen a bum before?"

Jozef heard the question, analyzed it, and came up with the only thing he thought would send this hobo away. "You like beer? Here's ten cents. You buy beer. You go. I busy. Thank you."

Ignoring the peace offering, the stranger blurted, "What's your name, old man?"

"Jozef."

"Jozef, you Slovensky—Magyar?"

"Ano, Slovensky."

The stranger immediately began to speak in Slovak. He explained to Stod that he was born in the Ukraine and spent time in Slovakia. Stod's eyes opened wide. He put the knife down and offered his countryman his leftover lunch. Jozef learned that this lump's name was Peter, no last name given. He had been riding the rails for days, starting from Pennsylvania and landing in Cleveland just today. He heard there were many Eastern European peoples here, and he wanted to settle down and find a job in the mills.

Stod became very comfortable with his new friend and opened up to him. They laughed as they both mispronounced each other's Slavic words comparing Ukrainian to Slovak. Stod told him his whole story of his crossing the Atlantic and settling in America.

Peter was very interested in every detail. The details that seemed to catch his attention most were Stod's butchering abilities.

"So you were a butcher in the old country?"

"Yes, and a good one too. Never did I waste a stroke. People in my village would come to me to slaughter the cows, pigs, and chickens."

"I raised rabbits for the table at home in Pennsylvania. Do you know how to dress a rabbit?"

"Rabbits are easy. Actually, all mammals go the same way."

"Tell me how you do it. Maybe I can pick up a few tips. You know, to make the job easier."

Jozef told how he never hunted rabbit in Slovakia, but on occasion he would be called to dress one. He told Peter a neighbor in his village raised rabbits, and when he died, he was asked by the widow to take the rabbits. She did not have the heart to kill them. There were a dozen in all. Some were springers, just right for the table. Stod went detail by detail into the description of the preparation. He told Peter how he would grab the rabbit by the hind legs and hit it in the back of the head with a piece of wood. This would stun the rabbit but not kill him. He would then cut off its head while the heart was still pumping and let it bleed out on the ground. Next he would cut off the rabbit's feet at the joints just above the paws. Taking the carcass, gripping the underbelly fur, he would slit the belly fur from the genital area up to its neck. He would pull the coat free from the body in one swift movement. A quick cut to the belly skin would expose the viscera, and he would carefully disembowel the rabbit. He cautioned Peter to be very careful with the bladder. One bad cut and the bladder would foul the meat. The intestines and genitals were also to be removed carefully so as not to poison the meat. Next the rabbit was then quartered and washed and made ready for supper. He used to tell his wife she could name the rabbits as long as their names were "dinner."

Stod saw Peter was noticeably taken aback by this gory mental picture. Stod thought, it was obvious Peter had never slaughtered anything.

"Well, old man, you sure know what you are talking about. That is exactly how I do it. Do you fry your rabbit?"

"Ano, bread, fry, and then bake it."

"Great, that's how I like to do it too." The man then said,

"So this is your project. You are going to make a garage out of this old boxcar wood. Mind if I look around?"

"No, go on. I need to start packing up. I have to haul this day's work up the hill to my house."

"You live on Manor?"

"Ano, 9600 Manor," Stod answered as if a child.

"Got a phone number?"

"No, son does though. Cedar 1-2324."

"I'm going to write that down. When I get a job I will call you. Okay?"

"Okay."

"Now let me have a look here. Maybe I can use something for my travels."

Peter went right to the bloody blanket. Stod watched him examine the bloodstains. He looked over the blanket inch by inch.

"What do you think happened here, Jozef?" Peter asked.

"I don't know. But I do know this blood is not a result of a small wound. Whoever did this bleeding is dead."

"Really?"

"Ano, look in the boxcar for the rest. It is a bloody mess in there."

Peter, belying his frail, gaunt, traveled look, jumped into the car.

Stod began to pile the day's wood onto the wheelbarrow.

Peter spent a long time in the boxcar. Minutes turned into an hour.

Stod finished his work and poked his nose into the car's door and saw Peter on his hands and knees scraping at the blood spot on the floor of the car.

"What you doing?" Jozef asked.

Peter shot up. "Nothing, just looking at all this junk in the corner."

"Well, I have to go now. Lena, my wife, will be expecting me soon."

"Do you mind if I help you take the wood home?"

"No, come on. Lena will have supper for us."

"One more thing, could I keep this old blanket? Looks like it would wash up pretty good."

"Go on. Lena would kill me if I brought that old thing home. She gets better from the Jewish ladies she cleans house for out in the Heights."

The caravan started up the hill, Stod pushing the wheelbarrow up the hill with Peter close behind. They did manage to stop at Kupcik's bar for a few. Stod introduced his traveler to his friends. They all had a merry time swapping tales about the old country.

As they left the bar, the *Cleveland News* truck pulled up and the deliveryman threw a couple of bundles of papers onto the sidewalk. Peter, once a paperboy, he explained, expertly cracked one of the bundles, pulling a paper from the middle.

The *Cleveland News* headline shouted, "Madman or Cool Killer? Police Probers Groping for Leads in County's Five Headless Murders."

Stod innocently asked what it said. Peter answered that the news was reporting another very hot day for tomorrow.

"If you are going to work on the boxcar tomorrow, you'd better get an early start."

"Yes, I intend to, but tomorrow's Sunday, no work. Today's heat taught me a lesson. End work well before noon."

The men arrived at the Manor home by three p.m., time enough to off load the wood, survey the garage foundation, and clean up for supper. Supper was always early if Stod was unemployed. Eat at four p.m., read the Slovak papers till six, sit on the downstairs porch with a beer or two until seven, and listen to the radio till eight, tuning in the rosary at exactly eight Say the rosary along with the radio and then off to bed by nine.

Today, Jozef's visitor interrupted the routine. The visit went smoothly for the Maders and Peter that evening. Beer started to flow and the bottle soon came out to the center of the table. Lena didn't like this but tolerated the drinking because of the guest. Peter was cordial, asking questions about the Mader's homeland and adopted city. The conversation went from Jozef and Lena's first meeting in the old country, the pigs, the butchering, landing in America, settling down in Cleveland, and the church.

"What church do you attend?"

"St. Benedict. Why do you ask?"

"Oh, just in case I want to settle in this area, maybe I would go to your church."

"But you are Ukrainian. Aren't you Orthodox?" Jozef inquired.

"Not all Ukrainians are Orthodox, Stod."

Stod hoisted his glass of whiskey and said, "Thank God for that."

The drinking and talking went well into the night. For every two beers or shots Stod had, Peter drank less. Right around midnight, after Lena was in bed for hours, the men decided to break off the party. Peter said half-jokingly that he had a train to catch, and if he missed it, there would be no refund on the ticket.

Stod laughed, gave him a great big bear hug, and showed him out. Peter was halfway down the driveway when Stod ran out to him. He kissed and hugged Peter again and gave him three bottles of beer, a pint of whiskey, and a couple of links of Kielbasa. This time Peter hugged and kissed Jozef. Stod followed Peter to the end of the driveway and watched him turn down the street and disappear into the night.

They were never to see each other again.

స్త్రీ ఌబ

The next morning the alarm went off at five. Father Leo got up, said his breviary, ate his breakfast, and walked over to the church to say seven o'clock Mass. St. Benedict Church was part of St. Benedict

School. Father Leo, the pastor, was always looking to save money and had built the school and church under one roof. His thrift would result in a million-dollar basilica some sixteen years later. His trek from the parish house to the church was a short one. He liked to get to church early. It gave him time to turn on the lights and open the windows to let some dawn-cooled air in.

Entering the church, he genuflected and made the sign of the cross. The light of this early summer morning flooded in through the stained-glass windows. He opened the windows and decided there was light enough, so he didn't turn the lights on. He worried about the light bill. As was his habit, he went in to the last pew on the right-hand side. He knelt and began to say an Our Father. He got halfway through the prayer when he felt a hand on his shoulder. He was startled. He turned to view a clean-shaven, dapper-looking man in a new suit, polished shoes, with a hat in his hand to complement his outfit.

"Excuse me, Father. Could I have a word with you? I need to know something about a man I just met yesterday. He is a parishioner of yours. His name is Joseph Mader. My name is Detective Peter Merylo of the Cleveland Homicide Unit."

It didn't take Father Leo long to convince Detective Merylo that Jozef had no connection with what would become the most notorious serial killings in the city of Cleveland and the United States at that time. The "Kingsbury Run Murderer" would kill a total of thirteen people by the end of his butchering spree. No one in law enforcement, let alone civilians, knew anything about mass killings, what would later be labeled serial killings.

⚜

In the end, Stod was able to keep the wood for his garage, less the bloodstained planks, from the back of the car.

Six months later the Slovak papers began to recount what was happening in Kingsbury Run. Stod followed the investigation to its unfinished end. He never spoke of the murders and the dark figure in his story until now. He knew he was part of Cleveland history. An ugly part.

Chapter 6
THE BUTTERFLY

J ozef told the group he was still scared to this day that the killer would come back to his neighborhood. He never returned to the railroad siding and cautioned his grandchildren not to play in the field next to the spur. That's all he had to do—tell them no. They spent many summer days down by the field, next to the tracks, the tracks of blood. His friends knew the impact this gruesome tale had on the psyche of this humble, simple man. A stronger person would have shrugged it off or even made jokes about his close call with death. Stod knew God saved him from a terrible death. He would thank God for his deliverance and be a better man. They never viewed that part of the neighborhood the same.

The year was 1965. It was a Saturday morning in the dead of summer. It was eight o'clock, and the sun shined in the front windows of the hardware store. The temperature in the front of the store was already eighty-five degrees. The pots and pans that lined the front window were hot to the touch. The spackling compound boxes stacked in a pyramid in the window were all faded. This was going to be one of those insufferable Cleveland days. The store was an oven. John would open the front and back doors for cross ventilation. Early Saturday morning and customers were already lined the center aisle.

John's sons Tom and Joel were fast at work. Tom, sweating, was cutting a key for a customer and Joel was fixing a window. The store was ripe. Turpentine, paint thinner, paint, oil from the pipe machine, and cigarette and cigar smoke polluted the air. The people in line patiently waited their turn. Most wanted to talk to John because he knew how to give simple advice about complex hardware problems. The discussions would lapse into Slovak or Hungarian as the need presented itself. As the customers stood in the narrow aisle, the talk would center on the Cleveland Indians—The Tribe. The All-star break was around the corner, and as always there was talk of pitching and pitchers for the second half of the season. Two younger men, up front by the key machine, were eying a beauty who had just climbed the steps of a CTS bus. The bus stop was right out the front door of the store. Her short shorts were the object of their admiration. Three older men were huddled in the center of the store and were whispering about the latest on Mrs. Janovick and her husband. John was explaining to Mr. Slavaczech how to replace a washer for a Chicago faucet. The hum of the store would continue all morning. Then for no reason, as anyone connected with retail could tell you, the rush fell off. No customers. It was break time.

John decided he would make one of his favorites for the Saturday crew: *canofle*. Canofle was a bread dumpling meal, what John referred to as Depression food. The mixed bread and eggs were fried in lard, rolled into a ball, and boiled in water. He was going to serve it with hot dogs. The final plate would be soaked in vinegar and cucumbers. This truly was heart attack food.

The chat group would slowly wander into the store. Milos, WWI vet and Stefan our WWII veteran, the bagman, Charlie, the cop, Anton, the construction worker, and Karol, the factory worker, rounded off the posse. Milos was especially animated today about something he'd read in the paper about the Catholic church.

"Well, the church is pulling people out of hell again," he declared sarcastically.

The last session of Vatican II was coming up in autumn. Some of the mysteries of the council of the three previous years were finally being published in the dailies. At first all the proceedings of this church get-together were closed to the public. It was rumored that some startling changes were afoot for the church faithful. Most of the everyday pew people didn't know a thing about what was happening. Nor did most care. Milos, our resident apostate, was always on the lookout for a chance to slam religion. The Catholic church was a favorite target. Of all the talkers, Milos was the least liked by John and his sons. He had a mean streak, and he would show it. He seemed to delight in cruelty. He once grabbed a cat by its tail and threw it up on the garage roof behind the store. He laughed and said, "If that's the worst I've ever done …"

"I don't know anything about religion, but I know what I believe," was Milos's mantra. Milos was raised Catholic, and like all searchers of the truth, became disillusioned with the religion of his youth.

"According to an article in the paper, you Catholics are going to be able to eat meat on Fridays," Milos shared with a smirk on his face.

It was as if the snake from the garden of Eden had slimed his way into the room and made this heretical pronouncement. John told Joel and Tom to go across the street to Square Deal and help their mother take groceries home. Mary always shopped on Saturdays, put the bill on the Mader tab, and had whatever sons were working at the hardware store help her with the larder.

"Don't talk like that in front of the kids," John said in not a very nice voice.

"I'm just telling you what your one holy, Catholic, and apostolic church has come up with again. More changes," Milos shot back, pleased with getting a rise out of John.

Stefan, Charlie, Anton, and Karol sat back, moaned, adjusted their seats, circled the two, and settled in for the battle.

"I don't care. You are not to talk about my church in that tone," John said, stepping toward Milos.

"Settle down, John. I won't pollute the little believers." Milos turned, making the sign of the cross with his left hand.

"Good," John said, hoping to end all discussion right there.

Stefan the intellect and devout Catholic wouldn't let it go. He enquired what the article's fine points were.

"Well, according to the article, Catholics will be allowed to eat meat on Fridays, except during Lent. If you eat meat on Fridays during Lent, back to hell you go," Milos said authoritatively.

"That's just the papers, they don't know anything. The church would never go against their holy doctrines." John responded with both eyebrows squished down in the middle of his forehead.

"Yeah," Stefan said, "what about all those people who went to hell without benefit of sacerdotal confession who ate meat on Fridays? The Church could never change course like that!"

"Ah, ha, wouldn't they though. The church changed its mind on priests marrying. Up to the twelfth century, priests were allowed to marry," Milos added argumentatively.

"Don't start again about the priests tying the knot, that's history," Anton interjected.

"Talking about those people already in hell for committing such a wrong as eating beef jerky or a piece of grandma's *hurka, rice sausage*, on Fridays, the article doesn't spill one drop of ink explaining what happens to them. Probably another one of those mysteries of faith. Going to hell because you ate meat at the wrong second on the wrong side of midnight on a Friday is absurd. What are the angels in the heavens keeping count with a stopwatch? Think about it. If we were to concede, for the sake of argument, that a thousand poor Friday flesh-eating souls were condemned to everlasting hellfire each year since the first Christmas, we could account for at least two million souls in flames (and we know there are many more fallen meat-eating souls in Christendom than that) if we were allowed to round off our multiplication. Now, continuing the argument, say the Church would grant a reprieve, and those slightly condemned souls were taken back to heaven, notwithstanding the moral problems, you have to figure at least forty thousand busloads (I don't know why counting angels on the tip of a pin was such a problem for the Church fathers; my religious calculations come so easy for me.), fifty in each bus. How would the Devil feel about all this? Holy mother, the Church has been such a grand ally for the Devil in history, the inquisition and religious wars and all that, now wanting to pluck his hard-earned, meat-eating sinful souls from hell would be a mean thing to do." Milos went on *ad nauseum.*

"I know the Church would never allow this. You are talking crazy. You are making light of a very serious law. Even if they did allow us to eat meat on Fridays, which they never will, I would continue to go meatless for God's sake," John said in a low angry voice. "Besides, it isn't the sin of eating meat that is going to keep those souls in hell but the sin of disobedience to Church law. God's law."

"God's law? Is the eleventh commandment the meat commandment?" Milos asked.

"Shut up! In this store, in my store, you will not mock Church law. It is the law of my Slovak ancestors. It is the law of my mother and my father. And I thank God that Stod is not here to hear this. It would break his heart to hear such talk." John's voice pronounced each word slowly to a crescendo.

The group followed the argument: knew John was angry; knew Milos made his points and was satisfied, at least, for today; they also knew that someone had to quickly change the subject.

"Who's hungry?" Karol asked. "Looks like the conofle is done."

"Can't eat without having a drink first," Charlie exclaimed as he reached for the bottle of whiskey, always handy under the back workbench.

"Thank Church law that drinking has never been forbidden on Fridays or any other day!" Milos shouted as he raised his glass to toast good friends.

"Ya, ya, Pravda!" the group chimed.

John, never one to hold an angry feeling toward anyone, soon began to smile. Besides, angry feelings were bad for business. This wasn't a barbershop, where religious talk could hurt business. They needed John and his steep discounts for his friends, and they were his friends. Besides, the entire group owed John money.

After everyone had a drink and began eating, Milos, very calmly and in a quiet voice, said, "Let's talk about a real mortal sin. I got away with murder."

Head hooded and down, hands tied behind a single wooden pole, legs bent, the body was crimson colored and torn, the work of a firing squad. The American squad of ten chose different parts of the body to do their work. One bullet hole in the hooded head. Hood removed, face gone. Parts of the skull and brain matter were embedded in the pole and hurdled on to the back stone wall. The retrieved skull was placed in the hood now serving as a bag. Shake the bag, hear the bones rattle. Four bullets to the heart, collapsing the chest. Four bullets to the stomach, releasing the intestines, pink and gray, dangling over the legs. One bullet to the groin, forcing the legs to spread, showing a five-inch hole where once was manhood. Blood, urine, and feces circled on the ground, formed a pedestal for the body, all adding to the odor in the air marking the freshly dead.

Milos was part of the firing squad and reluctantly a part of the cleanup crew. He was proud of his work that day. He just helped execute a Villista, one of Pancho Villa's soldiers. Cleanup would be easy but messy. It was a two-man job. A fellow squad member helped. The body parts were wrapped in burlap and carried to the camp dump. The burial ceremony was one quick heave of the purple package to the top of the garbage heap, kerosene poured on the body and set afire. He had done this before and knew enough not to stand downwind of the blaze. He kept the bloody hood with the skull bones as a remembrance.

This was the third month of the campaign of Black Jack Pershing's Punitive Expedition in Mexico. The year was 1916. The executions were never made public. There was no record of them in any official reports. They didn't happen often. It was known that Pancho Villa ordered firing squad executions of prisoners. With the Columbus, New Mexico, massacre of American citizens fresh in the memory of the US soldiers, executions in kind were carried out without the officers ever knowing. When they did find out about the executions, they condemned them but looked away.

Milos enjoyed the firing squad duty right from the beginning. He never puked after executions like the others. He slept well, no nightmares. He woke up the next day and was ready and willing to do it again. He wondered why he wasn't like the others. He was not sensitive to bloodletting. He came to this country from Zemplin in eastern Slovakia. He saw a lot. The Austrio-Hungarian police were not kind. He immediately joined the United States military: a way of eating daily. He was twenty-one years old and looking for adventure. He spent a week in New York boozing and whoring with his fellow recruits before being sent off to New Mexico to join General Pershing. Within six months of arriving in the states, he was a soldier in the Thirteenth Army Cavalry chasing the thug, Pancho Villa, around northern Mexico. He never thought he could hate anything or anyone more than the overlords of the old country. Three months of dealing with "the things," Mexicans, changed his mind.

Mariposa Rello was six years old, blonde, and a total delight to her parents. No one quite knew where this little sprite of a girl got her blonde hair and blue eyes. Everyone in the village of Parral was of a dark complexion. Her parents, although sunned like their fellow villagers, had a European look about them. Rumor had it that they were descendants of Basques from northern Spain. Gene pools play strange with humans. Mariposa's skin was ivory and her parents took precautions to guard her from the strong, brutal Mexican sun. Everyone in the village loved Mariposa. There were never any remarks about her hair or eyes or skin color. If anything, the villagers took pride in her difference. In church, she would stand out like a lovely flower. In a field of red roses, the white lily shines.

Mariposa, the butterfly, was true to her name. She would flitter from one activity to another. When given a chore to do, she would skip and sing through it. When she entered a room, it became cheerful and bright. Her father, Miguel, could not get enough kisses from her. When he came home from work in the fields, he would lift her up high over his head and kiss her all over. He would play a little game of kisses. Miguel would first kiss her left ear and give it a nibble and then kiss her lips and proceed on to the other ear for a kiss and a nibble. When she was younger, she allowed the kisses without interruption. Now that Mariposa was older, she would tease her father and not allow the sequence. One day, only the left ear. One day, only the lips. One day, only the right ear. Never two kisses in the row. She would keep moving her head back and forth until she became dizzy. Sometimes Miguel would try to kiss her for a half hour. When all was thought lost, she would grab her father by his ears and kiss both of his cheeks. Love could not be defined any better than those two at their kissing game.

Angel Rello, Mariposa's mother, thanked God every day for her butterfly. Mariposa was an only child and after six years, there were no others. This made Mariposa even more special. Instead of spoiling her, she made an extra effort to educate her. Most Mexicans could not read or write. Angel made arrangements with the nuns at church to go beyond religious instructions. She wanted them to teach Mariposa how to read and write. Every day Mariposa would go to the sisters' house for a lesson. She was a good student. In return, she would do little chores for the nuns. One chore she especially liked was delivering holy water to every household in the village. She would fill a gallon clay bucket with holy water from the baptismal fount in the church. Her father made her a small wheelbarrow just large enough to hold her precious cargo. House-to-house she would go, ladling out the sacred fluid into small containers on shrines made of crucifixes and candles. Each family would hug and kiss her and offer something to eat. Mariposa was too excited about doing God's work to eat. A short prayer and off Mariposa would skip to the next house. All was right in the world for Miguel, Angel, and the butterfly.

Milos could not stand going to Mass on Sundays when he was a child in Slovakia. It was boring and a waste of time. He never prayed or did anything religious without being forced. He would go through the motions of being religious, but he did not believe in God, the Catholic church, or any authority. Early in his childhood he met a freethinking Czech. The Czech polluted Milos with ideas, ideas that didn't make his parents happy. Eventually, Milos left his religion and his home and made his way to America. In America he transformed himself into a not so noble savage. Milos was free to do what he wanted. He became his own god. There was no right or wrong. With no parents or priest around to upbraid him, he did his sinning unabated. Drinking, whoring, and gambling filled his days. Joining the US military was a real stretch for him. He had to obey now.

Obey he did, when he was watched. Part of basic training was to become proficient in firearms. Milos took to this training. He loved to go to the firing range. He would be the first at the range. He was so good at finding the sweet spot on the target that the army even raised his monthly pay. Within weeks, he was asked to enroll in a special school for marksmen. His favorite rifle was the Springfield 03, what would come to be known as the 30-06. He could hit his target a thousand yards away with the new .30-caliber cartridge. Most marksmen had trouble at eight hundred and nine hundred yards. On a good day he could put ten consecutive shots in the bull's eye. Word of his accuracy traveled fast, and he was promoted to the advance guard in a sniper patrol. The army all but forgot about the importance of snipers. The lessons of the Civil War were forgotten. With all the head-on assaults in the Spanish American War, there was no need for snipers. In Mexico it was different. When the army decided to go deep into Mexico, they were confronted immediately by sniper fire from the Mexicans. Losses became painful. The Punitive Exposition was being punished. The Thirteenth Cavalry hastily assembled a squad of sharpshooters. Of the entire marksman in the unit, Milos became the "expert." He was the go-to man in difficult situations.

Putting a 30-06 rifle in Milo's hands had its problems. Everyone from the command down knew he was an angry man. Although he was an immigrant to the United States and spoke very broken English, he thought he was superior to the Villistas he was hunting. He was ready to kill all Mexicans. The problem was that not all Mexicans were members of Pancho Villa's gang. Direct orders from Washington clearly stated that only Villa's gang was to be held accountable. Pershing's men were not to provoke the Mexican regular army, the Carrancistas—Mexico's President Carranza's men.

The trouble was, Carranza's men were not behaving. They would thwart Pershing's mission whenever possible. The feeling was that the Americans were invading their homeland. Skirmishes between the regular armies happened all the time. Milos never cared who was shooting at him. He was out to kill: Villistas, Carrancistas, villagers, all brown people.

Milos, as a sniper, had a great deal of autonomy. He would go alone on most patrols. If he were accompanied, he would stick to his assignment. If alone, he would make the Devil proud of his actions.

"Milos."

"Yes, sir."

"I want you to scout ahead about three miles to see if you can locate the advance guard of the Carrancistas rumored to be active in the area," Major Jenkins commanded.

"Yes, sir," Milos answered in a crisp, military voice.

The area was about eighteen miles north of Parral. Parral was a village where supplies could be bought. Jenkins desperately needed to replenish his larder. Unlike Villa's men, who stole from the peasants, Pershing paid for all his supplies.

"I will do more than scout. Three brown pigs yesterday. Four brown pigs today. I will break my own record." Milos laughed in a low, muffled voice.

Two miles out and Milos spotted what was two black specks on a hill about nine hundred yards away. Within one minute, he was flat on his belly, tripod erected, rifle sighted, wind checked, shots fired. Dead black specks. He waited for a few minutes for his prey to bleed out and confidently walked the distance. His approach was nonchalant to the point of being merry.

He looked down on his brown prey and said, "Two more today to break my record." He searched the bodies for pesos, found a few mixed with family pictures. He pocketed the pesos and threw the photos in the air. He sat on the body of one of the dead Mexicans and wondered whether they were Villistas or Carrancistas.

"I really don't give a shit." Milos blurted.

At the three-mile mark, by his internal compass, he turned around because of his orders and headed back to camp. He didn't make his self-imposed quota of Mexicans today. He was sad. Orders are orders, and he could get into trouble for breaking them.

At the debriefing, he told Major Jenkins that he spotted two soldiers, but when he approached they disappeared over the horizon. Milos asked if he could go out alone again tomorrow. Jenkins said no because the detachment of 120 troopers were to march onto Parral in the morning, though his services would be needed soon.

ᴄᔆ ᕹᴐ

Mariposa's birthday, April 12, would be a day for celebration. She would be six years old. Preparations the week before took all of Angel's time. Close friends and neighbors would share the party, including enchiladas and *helado* (ice cream), Mariposa's favorites. Miguel made her a special piñata in secret. A real surprise. Invitations were passed out along Mariposa's holy water delivery route. Her tutoring that day would be cut short. The nuns would make this a special day for her. Cookies instead of books would be the order of the lesson. Although she would still replenish the holy water that day, she knew that each home would give her a special gift. The evening of April 11 was filled with anticipation. Mariposa was so excited she could not stop talking about the coming event. When she exhausted every particular of the party, she began to dream about her future. She told her mother and father that when she grew up she wanted to be like the sisters at church. She wanted to be a sister that was also a nurse. She wanted to help sick people for God. The rest of the evening she played dress up. She found an old blanket and wrapped it around her head and pretended she was a nun. She made all her dolls line up beside her bed to say the rosary. Mariposa would pretend that the dolls would make a mistake with their prayers and she would correct them. Half way through the medical portion of her fantasy, bandages on the knees of the dollies, wash clothes on the feverish heads, and salves on fresh make believe wounds, Mariposa fell asleep. Miguel and Angel slowly tiptoed into her room and quietly put the multicolored covers over her tiny body. They both kissed her. A short prayer and the home became silent.

⁂

That night, the Thirteenth Cavalry was bedded down a half-day's ride to Parral. Milos's orders were simple: leave early enough to get to Parral before sunrise with two Mexican scouts, find the tallest building in Parral, climb to its roof, and cover the Thirteenth Cavalry as it entered the town. Milos was the happiest man in the Thirteenth. The chance of killing some Mexicans was high. He loved the idea of sneaking in the dark into the town and setting himself up in a perch to kill unsuspecting birds on the ground. The Mexicans would be, ok, he said to himself laughing, sitting ducks. Milos knew, what every hunter knew, if you shot a sitting duck there would be nothing left of the bird.

The three headed out at two p.m. in the afternoon. Their expected arrival would be the next morning at two a.m. The ride was rough, but Milos barely noticed. He was like a kid anticipating a day at the circus. His Mexican companions thought there must be something seriously wrong with Milos. They didn't know what they would meet in the town, and they were scared. Milos was telling Slovak jokes in English, laughing, carry on like a schoolboy. When his buddies finally had enough, they asked him to shut up. For the last two hours of the ride Milos talked to himself. He kept repeating, "A church tower would be best … a church tower would be best."

When they entered the sleepy village under the cover of dark, Milos sent the Mexicans to two medium-sized buildings on opposite sides of the main street leading into the town. Milos found the bell tower of the only church in the village. The church sat on the far end of the village square. Main Street ended at the front door of the church. The church was open. He climbed the stairs and found his nest next to the tons of iron that hung from the ceiling of the steeple. How any melodic tone could come from that mass he would never understand. In the old country he hated the church bells. They were the Sunday wakeup call. After a Saturday of drinking, he resented going to church. *Damn the church,* he thought as he unbuttoned his pants to pee.

From his nest, he could clearly see his Mexican scouts on the roofs of the buildings. The sun came up, and their silhouettes were clear to Milos. They were just observers as far as he was concerned. In a firefight, they would not turn on their countrymen. They were useless to Milos. As he expected the church bell rang at six a.m.

sharp. He prepared for the ear shock by covering his ears with his coat. The town was up, but the regular business of the day seemed at a standstill. Milos didn't expect this. He heard Mass start below him at seven a.m. Around eight o'clock, when the stores were to open they didn't, and about a dozen small groups of two and three men formed in the square. The next chime would be at noon and by then his troops would be advancing to town. Did the villagers know this? The Carrancistas soldiers camped on the outskirts of the town were no threat to the Americans. Their orders were to let the Yankees go through the center of the pueblo unmolested. After all, they had a common enemy: Pancho Villa.

∽◉ ◉∾

Mariposa woke early on her birthday, all excited. Her mother put her hair up in two ponytails. Mariposa put on her best white Sunday dress. Her freshly shined shoes were put on, and a red rose was placed gently in her hair. The order of the day was to go to the church, greet the nuns, get the holy water for distribution, return home, and celebrate her birthday with her little friends and family.

"Mariposa, you look so beautiful. I am so happy for you I can cry." Angel sighed.

"My little butterfly, so delicate, so pure," Miguel proudly exclaimed.

"Where is your guardian angel?"

"On my right shoulder, Daddy!"

"Don't forget to show the sisters your new scapular."

"I won't mother."

The scapular medal was a piece of cloth with the image of the sacred heart of Jesus worn close to her heart. Her first present of the day.

"I love you, baby."

"I love you too, Daddy, but I am not a baby. I am six years old today!"

Mariposa skipped down the street to the church. She came to the plaza and was surprised by a crowd of townspeople. They were talking big people talk. Mariposa paid no attention to them and continued on to the sister's house. The nuns were full of joy this morning and showered Mariposa with cookies and candy and kisses. After fussing over her new scapular, they proudly sent her on her way to do her little duty. No tutoring class today. Mariposa, all smiles, cheerfully danced down to her first delivery house across the plaza from the church. She made her way with great difficulty through what became an unmanageable gathering. She sensed that the people milling around were angry about something. Mariposa heard the word "Yankee" spoken in a harsh way. She didn't know what the word meant nor did she care. This was grownup stuff that didn't concern her. She was too happy about the day's festivities to pay much attention. She just wanted to finish her holy chore and get home to celebrate. She looked up to the clear blue sky and praised Jesus for giving her such a beautiful day.

∽❀ ❀∾

The Thirteenth Cavalry was a mile out of Parral when Jenkins set up a meeting with the Carrancista General Lozano. Jenkins entered the town with his advance guard and met Lozano in the plaza. After a quick and formal greeting, Lozano said that his orders have been changed, and he would not allow the Thirteenth to go through the town. They would be allowed to re-supply and camp outside the town. Jenkins had no choice but to accept Lozano's proposal. The Carrancistas were not the bad guys. He wanted Villa and he needed supplies.

As the two finished their arrangements, the townspeople began to shout at the Yankee soldiers. The crowd pressed closer and closer to both the military men and their guards. Tempers flared. "Viva Villa!" and "Get out of Mexico, Yankees!" Shouts came to a crescendo. Lozano and his men formed a barrier between the Americans and the crowd. He pulled out his saber and ordered the Americans to proceed to the church and leave the town through the church alley. Lozano looked dead into the eyes of individuals in the group and knew that this was a serious mob. In an instant, the church bells sounded and firing started. The shots came from the mob. Lozano gave the order, and his men confronted the angry men. A Mexican officer fired his handgun directly into the mob. In fewer than a minute, all became chaos.

Milos observed the whole scene. Saw the puff of gunpowder from one man in the crowd. Took aim and fired. Congratulating himself on a clean kill, he took aim again. The second shot was not to be. The sound of a cocked gun next to his ear stopped this day's fun for Milos.

"Manos arribas," was shouted into Milos's ear. He turned slowly and was confronted by a Mexican soldier. Milos never heard the intruder's entrance because of the sounding of the church bells.

Mariposa lay dead in the street.

Her little white form, red rose still in her hair, was not discovered until the mob was dispersed. General Lozano was first to see her. She was lying next to her holy water crock with ladle in hand.

He dismounted, sat down next to this lifeless study, and picked her up in his lap. He yelled for a doctor. He knew it was too late. She was gone. He yelled again, half crying, "Does anyone know who this little girl is?"

"That's Mariposa," several in the crowd yelled together. Within minutes Mariposa's parents were given the terrible news. They came rushing to the scene. The sobs that came from Miguel and Angel pierced the heart of General Lozano. How could this happen? Who could have done this terrible thing? When the townspeople saw Angel take the precious little body from General Lozano and fall to her knees, forming a likeness of the Pieta, mournful sobs rose from the plaza. Where was Mariposa's guardian angel? What was God thinking?

Miguel immediately tore the front of Mariposa's dress to look for a gunshot wound. To his surprise, there was no blood, only a deep bruise, partially covered by her scapular, over her heart. The bruise was the size of a half dollar coin. Lozano's sharp eye caught a grayish colored object on the ground next to Angel's knee. It was a flattened spent lead cartridge. Medical science many years in the future would explain such a death. If a blow of sufficient force is applied to the chest, directly above the heart, the blow will interfere with the heart's electrical impulse and cause sudden death.

Mariposa had died of a gunshot wound.

Lozano picked up the spent cartridge and put it in his pocket. He got up and turned to the sound of his guards giving commands to a man whose hands were tied behind his back. Milos was under

Mexican arrest. Lozano needed time to sort out the terrible events of the afternoon. The soldier who captured Milos whispered to Lozano. Lozano's face turned a bright red. In anger, he told his guard to put the American in the town jail.

A funeral would take the place of a little girl's birthday party. A trial would be immediate.

General Lozano notified Major Jenkins that a Milos Janos was in the custody of a Mexican military court and was to be tried for double murder of two Mexican citizens, one twenty-one-year-old male named Juan Morales and one six-year old female named Mariposa Rello. The trial would take place the next day. Lozano made it clear that he wanted the major to be one of three judges. The court would be made up of two Mexicans, General Lozano, the mayor of Parral, and Major Jenkins. Milos could use any high-ranking officer of the US military for his defense. Lozano turned to the village magistrate for the prosecution. The courtroom would be a huge barn located between the two encampments of the Carrancistas and the Americans. A large crowd of hostile observers would attend the trial; the militaries of both sides would be expected to keep order. The court would convene at nine a.m. the next morning.

A mournful silence came over the village as they lay to rest the butterfly. Her wings would not flutter anymore, and the world was changed forever.

All Milos Janos could think was how the hell he had gotten caught.

The next morning the people of the village began assembling in the front yard of the barn, which was a huge horse shelter owned by a rich patron. Hay bales would serve as gallery chairs. The vaulted ceilings with a horseshoe loft covered a massive interior. The floor was made of cement. Horse stalls lined either side of the open floor. A large oak table was brought into the front to serve as a judge's bench. The judges would act as the jury.

The barn smells were unmistakable: horse manure, urine, hay, and oats. The spectators and military thought nothing of the familiar odors. Only late-twentieth-century man would be afraid of shit. The loft area would be filled first.

The villagers scrambled for the overhang and sat with their feet dangling over the sides. The ground floor, up front, was the place for the dignitaries: village counsel and the professional people. The whole area, top and bottom, held more than a hundred fifty onlookers. The yard and field around the barn held the overflow of another two hundred people. More than a hundred soldiers mixed in with this fold, like raisins in a loaf. The soldiers on both sides did not look happy. The scene was set for the opening arguments.

Santo Luz, the prosecutor, began by giving a concise history of the relationship between Mexico and the United States concerning the Punitive Exposition. He flavored his words with kindness. He complimented the Americans on their bravery for coming to Mexico to help bring Pancho Villa to justice. He repeated that the government of President Carranza was not the enemy of the United States. He went on to say all he wanted was justice for his village. He stated that the evidence would show overwhelmingly that the defendant, Milos Janos, committed premeditative, cold-blooded murder of two citizens of Parral.

Taking the offense, looking directly at the judges, Luz stated that no plea of innocence on the grounds of "inevitable military action" would be acceptable. Following orders of superiors would not carry this case. Santo Luz's description of the two innocent victims, Juan Morales and Mariposa Rello, opened floodgates of tears from the gallery. Below the tears were grumblings of a very angry mob.

Lieutenant Edward Adams, not a lawyer, but who had an extensive background in criminal military law, stood for Milos Janos. The audience immediately started to show its verbal dissatisfaction with the Yankee. The head judge, Lozano, had to threaten the gallery to maintain order. Adam's opening was nothing but complimentary to the Mexican side.

His praise was so profuse one would think the government of Carranza had been anointed by Jesus himself. Yes, he would show how Milos Janos indeed had fired his weapon, but it was not his bullet that killed the village's cherished citizens. Other gunfire had been heard. Janos was merely covering the rear guard of the military peace contingent.

When Adams finished, the crowd jumped up to attack Milos, who was sitting on a bale of hay in the horse stall closest to the judges. The soldiers, who flanked each side of the judges' bench, pointed their rifles, bayonets drawn, at the wild group. The judges all pulled their side arms, expecting the worst. One soldier pointed his rifle up to the ceiling and fired. The bullet went straight through the copula overhead and knocked the weather vane off the roof. The villagers outside rushed the barn door but were turned away by an armed guard of fifteen soldiers. A twenty-minute recess was called to calm everyone and to place two machine guns, one inside the court and another in front of the barn door. This move assured peace throughout the rest of the trial.

The first witness called by the prosecution was the soldier who had captured Milos in the church steeple. His name was Jesus Luiz.

"Mr. Luiz, would you please describe what you observed on April 12?"

"I was looking up at the bell tower of the church awaiting the noon bell when I saw a reflection of a ray of sun on something metallic. This was about ten minutes to noon."

"What did you do next?"

"I had to make a decision to move from my assigned post to get a better look."

"Did you?"

"Yes, there was no reason for anyone to be up in the bell tower. The bell was rung from a rope that fell two stories down to the bottom floor. I saw clearly a rifle barrel extended over the wall of the steeple."

"What did you do next?"

"I thought about contacting my sergeant to see if we had stationed a sniper in the church tower."

"Did you contact your sergeant?"

"No."

"Why?"

"I thought, if delayed, I would miss an opportunity for a stealth capture at the sounding of the noon bell. If the sniper was ours, nothing would be lost."

"What happened next?"

"I proceeded to slowly climb the steps up to the bell. When the bell began to strike twelve, I opened the trap door to the steeple in time to see the Yankee sniper shoot his rifle into the crowd below."

"How did you know he was a US soldier?"

"I could see at floor level he had on US military boots."

"Why did you arrest him?"

"Because there was no reason for him to fire into the crowd."

"Objection, Your Honors. Calls for speculation on the part of the witness. He clearly could not see what was going on in the plaza below."

"Overruled," Lozano said.

"What do you mean, 'no reason'?"

"The US military party was already safely out of harm's way."

"How so?"

"They passed me and headed down the alley next to the church."

"Was this before you went up to the steeple?"

"Yes."

"Nothing further of this witness at this time, Your Honors."

The audience rustled around in their seats and looked approvingly at their prosecutor.

"Your witness, Lieutenant Adams."

"Mr. Luiz, did you actually see Private Milos kill the victims?"

"No."

"Didn't you hear other gunfire as well?"

"No."

"Others heard more than one rifle shot. The total count was five rounds fired. You mean to state that you did not hear these other rounds fired? Can you explain?"

"Yes, I became totally deaf from the sounding of the bell."

"If you were deaf, how did you know Milos fired his rifle?"

"Easy—I saw smoke from the barrel."

"Milos, in his statement said he was smoking a cigarette. Could you have mistaken the cigarette smoke from the rifle?"

"No, I know the difference."

"How?"

"Rifles don't smoke cigarettes."

The crowd burst into laughter as Luiz was dismissed. The next witness called was Lozano's sergeant, Mendez, the soldier who had fired his handgun into the crowd of villagers.

"Sergeant Mendez, did you fire your weapon into the crowd on the day in question?" Luz asked.

"Yes."

"Did you kill Juan Morales and Mariposa Rello with a single shot from your handgun?"

"No!"

"How can you know for sure?"

"Because I didn't aim at my Mexican brothers and sisters. I aimed for the first O in the Coca-Cola sign on the wall behind my rightfully angry citizens. Go, you can see for yourself the slug is in the wall."

"Nothing further, Your Honors." Luz smiled as he sat.

The judges called another recess, this time for lunch and to remove the slug from the O.

After lunch and a siesta, court reconvened.

"Lieutenant Adams, would you like to cross-examine the witness?"

"Yes, Your Honor.

"Sergeant Mendez, how can you know for sure that this is your spent bullet that we retrieved from the wall? This could be a plant, a hoax."

"Your word against mine. But the bullet is .31 caliber—just like my handgun."

"Nothing further, Your Honors."

The prosecutor called three more witnesses. They were the men who had discharged their rifles to start the fray. They testified they'd shot their rifles in the air. The proof was no one was killed in front of them on the military line. Adams, clearly with his back against the wall, dismissed them and did not cross-examine. There was no point to it. The whole mess came down to "he said/they said." Adams, knowing Milos was a hothead who would probably wreck his flimsy case if he were placed on the stand, declined to have him do so. Two more witnesses were called.

"State your name, please," Prosecutor Luz declared.

"Jose Calandar."

"Mr. Calandar, is it true that you are a sniper and a scout for the US Military?"

"No, sir. I am just a scout."

"Mr. Calandar, do you hold any rank in the US Army?"

"No."

"Then why were you up in a building above the plaza with a rifle?"

"My Mexican friend and I, both scouts for the US Cavalry, were assigned to watch Milos Janos."

"Objection, Your Honors," Adams roared. "This is ludicrous. Are we expected to believe this?"

"Overruled," the mayor of Parral replied.

"What do you mean by 'watch' Milos?"

"We all knew, in our unit, that he liked blood, and he was only trusted to do what was right if his actions were observed."

The other Mexican scout testified that Milos was noted for enjoying the kill. According to the scout, most snipers did their jobs but did not relish the bloodletting. Both scouts testified that they saw Milos aim at the crowd and shoot at least one of the victims. On cross-examination, they both conceded that the shot from Sergeant Mendez's handgun could have been the fatal shot that killed the innocent people.

After a short recess, in which Major Jenkins conceded to his fellow judges that Milos was a hothead who needed special handling, the court began with a request from Luz. He wanted a scale, one that could measure down to grams.

Luz called for the bullet taken out of the Coca-Cola sign and one the equivalent weight of the 30-06 Milos used. Lozano said it was not necessary because he had the actual bullet that killed Juan and Mariposa. Adams objected, stating there was no proof that was the actual bullet. After Lozano testified that the flattened bullet perfectly matched the imprint of the bruise on Mariposa's chest, Adams reluctantly acknowledged the fact.

Luz called his next witness: Major Jenkins. There was a noticeable distraction of chatter in the gallery. How could one of the judges be a witness? The two other judges calmed the fears of an unfair trial by stating that Jenkins could only be used as a witness in technical military matters.

"Major Jenkins, only one question," Luz began. "Is there a

difference in weight of a spent bullet between a 30-06 and a .31-caliber handgun?"

"Well," started Jenkins.

"No explanation needed, just answer the question. Is there a difference—yes or no?"

"Yes."

"Is the difference noticeable?"

"Yes."

"How noticeable?"

"Three to one ratio in favor of the 30-06."

As Major Jenkins answered, Luz dropped the .31-caliber slug on the scale the lever tilted down to register its weight. The weight of the slug was recorded. The second 30-06 slug was also weighted. The proof was in the weight. The flattened slug found next to Mariposa's body was not .31 caliber.

Luz drilled even further, "Could a .31-caliber bullet do that much damage to a human body that was evident on Juan Morales?"

"No, if it was Jesus Luiz's bullet, it would have hit Morales's rib bones, entered into his chest cavity, and rested on the inside back rib cage."

"Why is that?"

"From the distance that the firearm was discharged, it would not have had the velocity to penetrate the body completely."

"Now, could Milos Janos's 30-06 have made these horrible fatal wounds."

"Yes," Major Jenkins, head bowed down, said in a low voice.

"Nothing further, Your Honors. I rest my case."

"The defense rests as well," Adams added.

In the summations, both officials of the court did a good job retelling their stories and bringing all the sympathy they could to their respective sides. Adams labored to paint Milos Janos in the best light as a protector of his superiors, a person who followed orders, and one who saw eminent danger and reacted accordingly.

Luz recounted what happened that day. He said Janos planned to kill some Mexicans. He was out for blood. He fired at the crowd after his soldiers were in the clear and out of harm's way, hitting Juan Morales in the chest. The bullet passed through Morales's chest, hit the ground, flattened and then ricocheted into the chest of Mariposa, the butterfly, killing them both. It was obvious that the bullet had come from Milos Janos's rifle. At the end of Luz's summation, the crowd was on its feet calling for revenge. If it weren't for the soldiers and the machine gun pointed at the gallery, they would have hanged Milos from a barn beam.

The judges went into recess to deliberate. The deliberation lasted thirty minutes. The verdict was unanimous: Milos was guilty of murder on two counts. He was sentenced to die by firing squad in the morning. "Blood shall have blood," Shakespeare wrote.

That night, Major Jenkins bribed the Mexican guards. Milos had been freed. Before sunrise he was on a Mexican train headed for Cleveland, Ohio, where there was a known Slovak community. He could lose himself in the large city, never to be found.

When Milos finished his long narrative, the group in the hardware store was stunned. They did not know what to say. In their midst was a murderer: an unrepentant killer. Finally recovered from the shock of the story, with all its underlying implications, Karol asked, "Milos, did you really kill those people in cold blood?"

Milos answered, "What's the big deal? They weren't people; they were Mexicans!"

Chapter 7
THE CHICKEN

J ackie came to the last page of her notebook, squinted, and said, "There, that's five thousand times." The sentence she wrote with all her heart, the heart of a thirteen-year-old little girl, was "I love Joey." It was September 1962. Jackie had Joey (Joel), who worked in his father's hardware store on Woodhill Road, and fell madly and deeply in love as only a teenage girl can. Joey, all of fifteen years old, was equally smitten.

Jackie was in study hall daydreaming about the past summer. It had all happened so quickly. She moved in above the hardware store in the corner apartment with her family. Jacqueline Eacott first saw Joel Mader working behind the store in one of the storage garages pumping paint thinner into gallon glass bottles. She remembered how he'd glanced up and said hi. That was all she needed to spark her quest. She wanted Joey to be her boyfriend, forever and ever.

It didn't take long for Joey to fall for her. Jackie was a tall, hazel eyed, beautiful brunette. Joey didn't have experience with girls. He went to Benedictine High School, an all boys' school. He was in the tenth grade and seriously thinking about joining the priesthood. That, of course, changed after the first kiss. They were inseparable. John Mader, Joel's father, took a liking to Jackie and allowed her to help in the hardware store. Jackie was pleased that Mr. Mader trusted her. The summer of 1962 was their summer of innocent love.

After the first time Joel talked to his love to be, he ran into the back of the hardware store and announced to the lunch crowd that he'd met "the most beautiful girl in the world." The men laughed and made the usual remarks about young love, first love. Joel told them to come out back and meet her. They dutifully followed his direction and went to check her out. The introductions were formal and lasted about two minutes. The factory whistles blew, and they had to go back to work. As they left, each one patted Joel on the head and said stuff like: "She's a keeper, great bedroom eyes, very grown up for her age." They all wondered, was she Catholic? Was she Slovak?

That September found Joel working in the Antel butcher shop on Saturdays for pay. John never paid his boys for working in the hardware store. He thought it was their duty to help the family. The cash would come in handy to go bowling or to the movies with Jackie.

Jackie would offer to shop for her mother at Antel's every Saturday morning. She needed an excuse to visit Joey. Unlike the hardware store, she couldn't just hang around the butcher shop.

That morning Mrs. Stofko was ahead of her. What followed would be a story that Joel and Jackie Mader would tell the lunch crowd and their growing family over and over again for years to come. The mere mention of the word "chicken" would call back memories of that September morning when their love was new.

There was never a family more particular about what they ate than the Stofkos. When Mrs. Stofko made breakfast for her family, it was an event. Take for instance something as simple as toast. The youngest son Stofko, Jack, would not eat his white toast if the crust was left on. Mother Stofko would dutifully cut off all sides of the bread. The oldest son Stanley would only eat it if the bottom crust were removed. Stanley's brother, Jeremiah, was a "top of the toast man." Remove the top of the crust and leave the rest and he would eat it. James Stofko, the father in the house, only ate the crust of the bread. The middle of the bread had to be removed. Besides his holey toast, he would eat all the others' crust leavings.

At lunch, all stops were pulled. Toasted cheese sandwiches, with all the peculiarities of the crust, were the selection of the day. First, the crust had to be removed as per above. One wanted the cheese on the top. One wanted the cheese on the bottom. One wanted the cheese in the middle slightly melted, but not leaking over the edges. James, the old man, of course, wanted his with no middle bread, but the cheese wrapped around the crust of the bread.

When it came to the favored beverage, tea was tops on their list— tea in various strengths and color and every kind imaginable: really weak; medium weak; and just plain weak; a little strong; medium strong and undrinkable; yellow; green; dark; and light.

Just imagine what a full-course dinner was like for Mrs. Stofko. She would have to start cooking at six in the morning if she wanted to finish in time for supper. Her planning a dinner menu was like a general planning a full-out assault. The only difference is the general doesn't have to worry about pleasing everyone. Mrs. Stofko decided on chicken for today's supper. This necessitated a trip to the neighborhood butcher shop.

John Antel's butcher shop was two stores south of Mader Hardware. John Mader would buy all his chuck roast meat for his famous soup from Antel. Antel was Hungarian, but John liked him. There was an unwritten rule that all the merchants would patronize each other. Antel was a small man but was built like he could throw a side of beef the length of a football field. He spoke with a heavy accent that would confuse any unsuspecting little boy who went to the shop without a list. The shop was like all corner butcher shops in Cleveland.

Just like the hardware store, sale-of-the-day signs were taped on the front and in the center of the window of Antel's shop. Bologna was on sale for nineteen cents a pound. This week's special, luckily for Mrs. Stofko, was whole roasting chicken. On the rack in the window were coils of smoked kielbasa and hurka hanging next to pork fatback. A tin bell rang when you entered the front door of the shop. Once in the butcher shop, the smell of garlic hit you so hard you could taste it in your mouth. The wood floor, in front of the fresh meat display counter, was dotted with sawdust foot tracks. The refrigerated counter ran parallel to the shop walls with an opening by the front door. A vat of pickled herring sat in the front window close to the door for easy sampling. The small freezer was lodged next to the display counter and ran perpendicular to the back wall. This was a time before frozen foods became popular. The back wall was the side of the huge wooden meat cooler where sides of beef hung, and crates full of chickens were stored, and various ethnic meats were cured. In the front customer area, shelves held bread and buns for sandwiches. Condiments held a prominent spot in the middle of the shelves. Canned soups were located at the end next to the freezer. The meat display case contained so many different cuts, it was only with the help of John, the butcher, that a costumer could circumnavigate the offerings.

Behind the huge counter, tin signs advertising bread and milk, bacon and eggs, and brands of meats were nailed to the wall. The floors in this area were covered with an inch of sawdust. The shavings acted as a sponge to soak up the fat carvings that fell to the floor. Because of the sawdust, fat was unable to adhere to the floor and make lumps like chewing gum. This, of course, explained the sawdust footprints in the front of the counter. The length of the display counter on the butcher's side held a small eight-inch wooden counter for wrapping the meat packages. At the back of the counter was an old-fashioned cash register designed specifically for the shop. The register rang with every sale. The sound was so distinct that once you heard the sound, you never forgot it. The hunger reflex was aroused when the bell rang. The register was good for business. Behind the register as the lunchmeat slicer and a small wooden butcher block. This block was used to dress the meat and cut off excess fat if the costumer requested.

The back of the butcher shop was where the serious butchering happened. As you walked through the backroom door to the right was the big band saw. In front of the band saw to the sidewall was the huge industrial-size six-burner black gas stove with a large vent hood above. This stove was the workhorse of the shop. All cooking for various sausage meats was done on its massive burners. On the back wall was a stainless steel table where the fresh and smoked sausage was made. Next to the cooler on the left side was another butcher block, twice the size of the one up front. This block was used for serious butchering. The block could accommodate a quarter hind of beef. Lastly, in the basement of the shop was the smokehouse, the last stop for the delicacies before they were hung in the front window. The smokehouse filled the neighborhood with the aroma of the gods. The last thing on the mind of an old Slovak about to expire would not be a "rosebud" sled but the odor of John Antel's butcher shop smokehouse.

Unlike the hardware business, the butcher shop did not lend itself to loitering. Because of health laws, costumers could not go behind the counter and chitchat. There were no seats in the customer area. Yes, there was talk and gossip in the shop but limited to the time it took the butcher to fill your order. Everything was cash and carry. Sales happened quickly. Customers hated to wait a long time for their turn. If the butcher was too chatty, one could always go down the street a couple of blocks to a more efficient and less gregarious butcher. It is in this shop that Mrs. Stofko decided to buy her whole chicken.

Mr. Antel saw Mrs. Stofko waiting by the light across Woodhill Road. It took all his might to stop himself from putting the closed sign on the front door. His Saturday helper, Joel, was in the back cutting lung meat for the hurka. When Mrs. Stofko—Beta—came into the store, a crowd of costumers followed. She was first in line, Jackie, Joel's girlfriend, was behind her. Mr. Antel had to wait on her. Joel was safe this time. He would wait on Jackie, very convenient for the lovers.

"Can I help you, Beta?" Antel asked.

"Yes, I would like to have a large roasting chicken please."

"You are in luck; chicken is on sale today."

"Could I please see one?"

"Here—we have a beautiful, fresh chicken saved just for you, Beta."

"Okay, let me see; I have my list right here. My son, Jack, only likes the wings of the bird. Well maybe not both wings." Quizzically staring at the chicken, she added, "Yes, that's it. He only likes the left wing. That is usually the fatter and stronger of the two. Everyone knows chickens use their left wings more than their right wings. But Jack doesn't like the right wing cooked in the same pot with the left wing. He claims it taints the meat. You'd better cut both wings off and throw them aside."

Antel sighed, cut the wings off the body of the chicken, and held it up once more.

"That's fine," Beta said approvingly. "Now, you know my Stanley loves breast meat. He is definitely a breast man."

Joel and Jackie, taking this all in, began to laugh out loud, as did all the other costumers in the store.

Mrs. Stofko, so deep in concentration, was not aware of the laughter. She just continued.

"Yes, Stanley loves big breasts. But you do know, Mr. Antel, he only likes the right breast of the chicken. He says chickens always show their left breasts to the sun when they are out feeding in the poultry yard. Sunrays are cancerous, and Stanley refuses to eat left breast meat in fear of getting cancer. So please cut that left breast off the chicken and throw it away."

Antel did as he was told, again holding the less-than-complete chicken up one more time for Mrs. Stofko's viewing.

"Now my Jeremiah loves thighs but will not eat them if they ever touch the legs of the chicken. He is definitely not a leg man. So it goes without saying, you need to cut the legs and thighs off the bird and throw them away too!" Beta explained in a calm, almost apologetic manner.

Antel again reduced the bird by two drumsticks and thighs.

"Well, that leaves my James. He just loves to suck on the neck bone of the chicken; that is, if it never was connected to its right breast. No, that would never do. Please remove the neck and right breast."

Nonplussed, butcher John held up the only part of the chicken that was left and said, "I hope your boys are 'ass' men because that's all that's left of the poor chicken."

Mrs. Stofko, very pleased with herself, responded, "I'll take it. Wrap it up. You know my boys are not particular about what they eat!"

Chapter 8
THE ASYLUM

Milos Janos died in 1966. To anyone's knowledge, he died unrepentant of his mortal sins. Mrs. Stofko had a stroke, so her sons and husband had to cut the crust off their own bread. Unbeknownst to John Mader and his family, the hardware store would close forever in just three years. The store had not really changed much in the last twenty-two years. All was right in the world of Cleveland, Ohio, on Woodhill Road. Above all, the hardware store was a democratic refuge. John never turned anyone away.

J. D. and Bernie were on the lowest step of society's invisible ladder. J. D., a middle-aged man from West Virginia, was tall and lanky with a head vacant of teeth. J. D.'s mind was mostly gone. Rumor was that a mule had kicked him in his youth. His skull was fractured and a metal plate replaced the bone. What he lost in brainpower he made up in personality. His favorite pastime, in the winter, was to come into the hardware store, stand over the heater vent, and "suck up the heat." As he warmed himself, he greeted the customers. The customers knew J. D. and were used to him. On days when he was absent, customers would ask John where J. D. was.

Bernie was a short man who liked his wine. He would come into the hardware store and beg for pennies. Bernie's smile would melt the heart of John's customers, and they freely gave him their loose change.

J. D. and Bernie were just two examples of gentle souls who came to an end at the Northern Ohio Lunatic Asylum. Woodhill Road would give many a soul to the eerie building with its dark towers.

The store was vacant of customer traffic this day in the winter of 1967. It was Monday, and Mondays in the winter were always slow. The group that came together in the back of the store was different today. Added to the regulars were Dr. Andrisek and lawyer Drabik. The doctor and the lawyer tried to make it at least once a month to the gathering. The discussion this day centered on the Vietnam War. Like all military-political discussions, with its pros and cons, nothing was resolved. The discussion was abruptly interrupted by Stefan, our bagman, entering through the back door, agitated about the abuse of his brother by the attendant staff of the asylum on Turney Road. Turney Tech, as the asylum was known by anyone who lived within a five-mile radius, was an old hospital for the mentally ill. Stefan's brother, Alex, was autistic and lived in the asylum for many years. This time the group was unable to calm "Steve" (Stefan's American name). They were usually able to quiet him so that he would not go into a harangue about his brother. No one wanted to hear about the "loony bin" again, another slang name for the once Newburgh Lunatic Asylum. Steve's stories of the hospital were stale. But this time, Steve was more than excited. He was wide eyed and scary looking. There was almost something supernaturally weird about him, like he had seen a specter. It was obvious that something had happened to Steve that forced his otherworldliness appearance. The lawyer and the doctor were especially interested in his transformation. They both asked him, not as a client or a patient but as a friend of a close group that bonded in the back of the hardware store: what was wrong? The answer to that question was "everything." He was reluctant to tell what happened this last week at the asylum. They probably would reserve a room next to his brother in the nuthouse if he let out what happened. He was confused. His story began forty years earlier.

Alex had a fitful sleep in the bedroom off the parlor. This early November night in 1927 was not unlike other November nights in northern Ohio. Winter was already showing its ugly head a month and a half before its official arrival. It snowed almost a foot that day. Just two days before it had been in the '70s. Alex was the youngest of four children in this Hungarian family. Fred was the oldest, then Steve, and then Anna. The parents, Luke and Martha, put Steve in charge of ordering the coal for the winter. The coal was dumped a ton at a time in the small backyard of the Hadarich house on East Ninety-Second Street, three streets down Sophia Avenue from Woodhill Road. The backyard was fenced except for a gate big enough to allow a coal truck to dump its black energy close to the house. The small cast-iron plain coal stove stood in the interior corner of the parlor. The parlor of this tiny hundred-year-old immigrant home sat in the middle of the house. The back door entrance opened to a small kitchen and bathroom. The kitchen had an early twentieth century look to it. The sink was made of wood. The dirty brass faucets were separate spigots: one hot and one cold. The hot water came from an old sidearm galvanized hot water heater in the corner of the kitchen. The table that stood in the center of the room was ornate porcelain with wooden legs. The table had one matched chair; the other three were castoffs from the garbage. A picture of the Last Supper hung next to a holy water dish on the wall next to the entrance to the parlor. A single door-less cabinet, for pots and pans, was under the sink. The stove was a coal burning, black, four burner that exhausted through the roof.

The original black pipe that ascended from the back of the stove was gray with use. The bathroom, the size of a small closet, suffocated a copper bathtub with an old-fashioned, high hung reservoir water tank toilet with a chain pull to flush.

The parlor lovingly held the comfortable furniture of the house. Two rocking chairs occupied the best space in front of the heating stove. A two-seat sofa, threadbare on its arms, was pushed up against the two side windows of the room. A round rug in the center of the room would be the younger children's special place. The front room, rarely used, held the proud mementos from the old country. The front door of ordinary wood and skeletal lock was to the right side of the room. This door led to the front wooden porch. Pictures of long dead relatives and of biblical scenes decorated the wall. A family portrait, showing the proud mother holding the newborn Alex in her arms, was prominent. Because of poor teeth, no one smiled. The only furniture in this room was a cherished Windsor rocker and a large austere oak table that look too large for the room. In the center of the table, was a gold crucifix sitting on a white dainty doily. Anna, the young daughter, was continuing the art of crocheting old country doilies. When she grew older, she would spend her days as a seamstress in a precious stone polishing cloth manufacturing sweatshop.

The second and last bedroom was right off the front living room. A colorful red and green drape depicting the crucifixion served as a partition between the rooms. Three small single horsehair mattress beds nestled into a space made for one. There was no room for dressers. The outerwear clothing was stored on the floor at the foot of each bed. Shoes, underwear, and personal items were stored under the beds. A rosary lay on each pillow. The floors throughout the house were made of white pine and gave off slivers. The house was hot in the summer and cold during the winter.

Alex's fitfulness turned into a full-blown fever that reached 105 degrees measured by the only medical item the Hadariches owned: an old mercury thermometer. At first Luke and Martha thought it was a minor cold fever that would pass. When night came and then day and the fever would not break, they became worried. There was no money for a doctor. Home cures were applied. No results. Martha and Luke took turns holding and rocking the hot precious bundle. Another day went by and their little angel continued to burn. They knew they were going to lose Alex. Fred, Steve, and Anna huddled around their brother on the cold parlor floor where Mother had placed Alex. They said goodbye. The almost lifeless form looked up at father, Luke, and stopped breathing.

Martha grabbed the baby in her arms and rushed out of the

back door of the house and carefully laid her son in a snow bank. Luke and the children ran after her in disbelief. Martha covered the baby in snow. Steam rising off the snowdrift gave testament to the awful pain and high temperature of the child. The family cried in confusion. A well child just two days ago had become a steaming corpse in the snow. Father told the children to go back into the house. He was going to build a small wooden box to place Alex in until arrangements could be made. Mother took Anna and her brothers into the parlor, stoked the stove, and cried the cry of a sorrowful mother. Deep were her groans. They seem to come from her bowels: a mournful, otherworldly sound. The children cried with her. All was lost.

Father Luke went to retrieve some wood from apple and orange crates stored under the back of the house. When he returned to the steaming pile of love and knelt down, the dead child's hand shot up through the top layer of snow right in his face. Startled, Luke fell back on his tailbone and gave out a cry. Quickly recovering, he carefully removed the snow from the dead child to find a breathing infant. He screamed with joy. Martha and the children came running from the house to see a living child. All was not lost! The fever had broken and the child was alive. Martha pick the baby up and held it close to her breast. She could feel its little lungs filling with air. A rosy pink hue came back to its round cheeks. A strong heart pounded against its now moving chest. At that moment, the sun came up and shined on this family of fortune. She raised the little cold frame to the heavens and thanked God for his miracle. There would be rejoicing in the Hadarich family that night.

Alex, across from the wood-burning stove, stared into the fire. Saliva drooled down the sides of his mouth. He was ten years old now. This was his daily routine.

"Luke, we must take him back to the hospital. The hospital has a new superintendent. The rumor is that he has a new treatment for mentally sick children. Please, let's give it another try," Martha pleaded.

"I am not going to waste another dollar on Alex's treatment. Martha, he is brain dead. He was deprived of oxygen too long when he almost died of that fever. The sooner you realize there is no hope, the better it will be for all of us," Luke replied in a slow but loving reply.

Alex was dead—dead in a world that was alive. He could not talk. He did not interact with his family. Eating seemed to be a reflex. He did not respond to any stimulus around him. His days were spent sitting in the parlor staring at the wood stove. In the summer, Martha would walk him out to the back of the house, and he would sit and stare at the ground. Yes, Alex was brain dead during a time when the medical profession knew very little about autism. Martha and Luke knew if they sent him to the mental hospital, Alex would be locked away in a room. They both loved what was left of Alex. He was their child and he had a soul.

Steve was drafted and went to war. He left Alex in his family's care. Soon after his return, his parents died. Anna, Fred, and Steve became custodians of Alex. Steve, although well read and brilliant, was never quite right after the war. He could only hold down menial jobs. The job that lasted the longest was dishwasher for the Italian bakery. Tardino's Bakery shared a common basement hall door with Mader Hardware. John Mader and Steve Hadarich went to school together from kindergarten to sixth grade at St. Ladislas School. They were lifelong friends who fought like brothers. Steve's nickname for John was "Fitzle." John had a nickname for Steve. He was pain-in-the-ass Steve. John, betraying his soft side, would always ask about Alex's progress. Steve knew John was a good man, and he would tell him the worst about Alex's behavior.

There really was no "worst" behavior. Alex was just there. Even when he was finally institutionalized at the Cleveland State Hospital, he gave no indication that anything different happened. It was sad for the family to send him "off." But it wasn't that sad. Steve took it the hardest because he was the one who was closest to Alex. He would change his diapers even as an adult. It was the coming of age, in this case, Alex turning twenty-one in 1947 that cause the moved to the asylum. With Fred and Anna working all day, one person could not manage Alex because of his weight and height. Alex began smoking cigarettes at age eighteen. It was the only thing that seemed to give him any pleasure. The risk of a fire in the little house was ever present.

In the beginning, Alex was first given a room in the men's wing closest to the main building. Really, Alex was nothing special to deserve a place in the elite section of the mental hospital. All patients, when they first arrived, were placed close to the doctors in the main section of the building, the administration section, the tower section. This was a holdover from the philosophy that all mentally ill persons could somehow be cured by special treatment in a month. It was immediately obvious to the staff that there would be no cure for this autistic, non-verbal, and brain-dead person. The mere fact that he was quiet and not aggressive bought him a stay close to the tower. Only loud, aggressive, non-paying, homeless alcoholics and dope attics were thrown into the far reaches of the wings. No one could hear them if they were roomed in the no-man's land of the locked secured wings farthest away from the doctors and visitors.

The famous Kirkbridge-type hospital, with its huge, two tower, castle-like administration and receiving building with wings of rooms and dormitories branching out either side, was the darling design of the nineteenth century. The superintendents of the middle nineteenth century actually believed that the physical plant of an asylum was a major factor in the cure of mental patients. The location, always in a rural setting outside the main city was the best environment for these hapless victims of broken minds. Turney Road, west of Garfield Heights, was just such a setting. The corridor of the wings would sometimes be built with only rooms on one side, so windows could be opened and good clean country air would flow freely. Late in the nineteenth century the cottage movement was introduced. Hospitals began to think that if patients of certain degrees of mental illness were placed in small houses outside the main building, they had a better chance of being cured. The Turney Road Hospital began erecting outbuildings to accommodate the new thinking.

Zelda Adams was a heartless and soulless. Adams was in charge of the ward that housed J. D., Bernie and Alex. Zelda was a holdover from at least three administrations spanning forty years of her life at what was now known as the Cleveland State Mental Hospital. Her mother and grandmother, going back to the nineteenth century, were also nurses at the lunatic asylum. She was nasty even as a child. In kindergarten she would throw classmates into mud puddles just for kicks. By the eighth grade she was tattling on her fellow students for necking and smoking behind the curtain of the school auditorium. Zelda was the walking realization of the "old crabby person," who had been a young crabby person. Ugliness was in her genes. People change. Not this one.

Alex was the first to arrive at the hospital, followed by J. D. and then Bernie. All three, over the years, were subjected to all sorts of treatments. They had been through every therapy imaginable: primitive drug therapy, electric shock therapy, and environmental therapy, cognitive psychological therapy, Freudian therapy, and occupational therapy. They roomed together in an overcrowded dormitory. Alex's room's prime location, close to the administration building, came to an end when the hospital became overcrowded. The three were sent to the far reaches of the men's wing where the worst patients were. The "Woodhill Road Three" were all pretty much out of it by the time they entered this faraway wing, Alex, never right because of the fever, J. D., who finally succumbed because of the mule kick, and Bernie because of the drink. All three were no longer verbal. The one thing they had in common, beside their illness, was they all came from the neighborhood around the hardware store, and Steve would check on them with a visit almost every day.

Steve, the bagman, would go to the grocery store in the morning and take the bus from Woodhill Road to Ninety-Third Street to Turney Road to the hospital in the evening. On Sundays, Anna and Steve would visit the asylum and then later stop at Calvary Cemetery to visit their mother and father's graves. This routine went on for years. Steve got to know the staff of the hospital well. Because of his daily visits, the less-than-kind staff members kept their mean hands off Alex, J. D., and Bernie. The staff knew a watchful family member and friend would surely cause trouble if something happened to their patient. Over the years, Steve became known as a troublemaker. The trouble he made was the demand that the staff did their jobs: a demand that government workers did not understand and resented. Steve and Zelda Adams never got along.

Yellow smelly pee was everywhere: in beds; on the floors in the rooms; in the hallways; and on the patients' chairs. The stench of human urine was everywhere. This was a hallmark of sanitarium living. Zelda used pee as a tool. If she didn't like a patient, she would have the patient sit in his urine for days. Besides the smell, the urine would cause all kinds of discomforts for the abused. Rashes and bedsores followed by infection, which could result in death, was the future for these poor souls. Failure to thoroughly clean the soiled human charge was another way of getting back at the outcast.

Caked, hardened excrement in the pants of a patient would turn the most recalcitrant patient to see the light: Zelda's light. None of these softening methods could be used on the Woodhill Three because Steve kept a watchful eye on his brother and his friends. Sure they smelled. Biweekly baths will do that for you. It could have been worse. Never wanting for ways to torture her patients, Zelda would just reach deeper into her bag of terrible tricks to come up with alternative ways. She would find what the person cherished most and deprive him or her of it. That worked.

"Mr. Hadarich, your brother continues to disobey me in regard to his cigarette smoking. I have told him repeatedly not to smoke in his dormitory room," Zelda Adams scolded.

Adams always spoke in terms of "in regard to" or "is there a reason for" and "how can we," always trying to dress up her verbal assaults. What she meant was she didn't like something and she wanted it changed.

Adams continued, sounding like a nun confronting a fifth grader: "I will not tolerate this conduct. If this continues, I will be forced to take his smoking privileges away."

There it was. It didn't take long for Zelda to enforce her threat. The one thing Alex found pleasure in—gone. Gone too was J.D.'s chewing tobacco and Bernie's lucky penny he liked to pitch against the wall. Zelda smoked and chewed and what the hell, a penny is a penny. She thought she deserved these perks. Of course, Steve would replenish the tobacco supplies and the penny at each visit. As conscientious as Steve was, the burden of keeping up with Zelda's demands was daunting. Tobacco was cheap. Replacing a penny was easy, but over time, it became the principle of the thing. Why should she have a free ride? What was Steve to do? Complain? To whom? The asylum's population overwhelmed the doctors in charge. They were not about to side with a relative about something as trite as some missing cigarettes. The nurses did all the dirty work. They deserved a few free butts. Steve let it go. But the Woodhill Three did not. Any chance they had, they would devise a prank to upset her.

Crouched in their favorite corner of the dorm room, off away from all the hassles of the other patients, Alex, J. D., and Bernie sat in their own smell and stared at each other. Their stares were not blank looks. There was a form of communication happening. To an outsider, nothing seemed amiss, just three autistic patients looking dumb. Steve, at times, would have a suspicion that more was going on than just three bunkmates staring at each other. Steve would never tell anyone what he thought. Were they actually communicating? Who would believe?

"The witch took my cigarettes again," Alex scoffed.

"My chew too!" J. D. said.

"A penny lost is a penny lost," Bernie added.

"Z could look up my butt for honey for all I care," Alex said. They called Zelda "Z."

"Yeah, she could crawl up my butt and have a picnic," J. D. added.

"A lucky penny short is not luck, witch," Bernie said.

"I got her back. I hung a piece of toilet paper with shit on it in the women's bathroom. When she opened the door, she got shit on her face," J. D. gleefully announced.

Alex went on. "Have you noticed she is not like us? Look at you, J. D. There is a bright light around your head with little black spots here and there on the light—like a mourning wreath."

"Yeah, you and Bernie have lights too."

"Wow, my light has more dark spots than both of yours," Bernie said.

"Have you both noticed that Zelda Adams doesn't have a light? Maybe her black spots block out the light?"

Alex continued. "I never noticed it before now. I just thought all of us had the light."

"Quiet, here comes the witch now," Bernie interrupted.

Zelda, wiping her face of the shit with her nurse's apron, pounced into the dorm unannounced. Revenge is what she had on her mind. Immediately, she saw Alex in the corner sitting with his buddies and smoking. Without warning, with a closed fist, she punched Alex in his head. The blow knocked him to the ground and he began to bleed from one of his ears. On the ground face up, Alex began banging his head on the cement floor. Blood flowed. Bernie and J. D. became agitated and threw chairs and turned beds over. Arms and feet flailed. An alarm sounded and guards from all over the asylum came to help settle down the wing. The dorm became extremely bright with a blinding light. So many bodies entwined together, so much light coming from their heads. Light that only the Woodhill Three could see.

Mental illness can cause extremes in behavior. The violent side of person can explode for no reason. Usually the violence is inwardly directed. Alex never hit Zelda back. J.D. and Bernie never intended to throw the chairs and beds at anyone. Alex hit his head repeatedly on the ground, hurting only himself.

Zelda wasted no time accusing the three of breaking the rules. She made up a story of how Alex had attacked her and how she'd had to defend herself. J.D. and Bernie were equally at fault. They'd jumped her too. Alex, Bernie, and J.D. were transferred to the bowels of the building and were not allowed visitors for a week. During the night, they were bound to their beds. During the day they were given no food and water only every other day.

The trip to the basement of the men's wing would have been eventful to a student of antique architecture or a devotee of Edgar Allen Poe. At the end of the hall, close to the vestibule of the main building were two white doors that swung inward to reveal a bank of steam heat and paint peeling from the radiators. Windows above the radiators opened to the main greeting hall, exposing a pristine world far different from the outer wards. No urine smell here. A long walkway, encased with windows reaching from the floor to the twelve-foot ceilings on each side, showcased the entrance to the lower level. High iron arch supports placed equally distant from the beginning to the end gave a medieval cathedral look to the area. The walls of the staircase that led to the dungeon were blackened with fingerprints of unfortunate inmates that went for this same walk. One hundred years of use left a graphic reminder of the region below. The wrought iron staircase that was the portal to the nether region didn't so much as descend down as plunged down. The stairs were steep, and if a patient happened to slip, oh well! The hurtful fall would just make him more pliable.

The base floor of the cellar consisted of a series of tunnel corridors opening up into larger rooms. Most of the rooms were utility rooms. Some housed phone block switches, furnace rooms, and huge electrical boxes. The padded cells and electric shock rooms were found here as well. These were smaller rooms directly off the corridor. They resembled prison cells. The cells would house as many as four beds. The corridor reached from one end of the asylum to the other. Tunnels veered off under each of the wings. Locked massive wooden doors segregated the cave-like passages. Each door had a nineteenth-century skeleton key lock. The keys were large and made of steel. Each of the keys was numbered showing the wing and section of the building you were under. To service anything in the basement, a repairman would have to have as many as ten keys to get to where he needed to be. It was a phone repairman's nightmare.

If the Woodhill Three were aware of their surroundings, they would have smelled the dank, wet mold that clung to the century-old brick and stone foundation. They would have seen rat holes chewed on the corner of each wooden door showing an unobstructed highway made by the nasty rodents. They would have heard the otherworldly wailing of the inmates in the padded cells. They would have heard the screams of the electric shock patients. They would have sensed the terrible tragedies of hundreds of ordinary, not so sane people, who were housed here.

Alex, J. D., and Bernie were thrown into one of the rooms closest to the pump room that forced the sewage out into the mains. The leaky sewer vents transversed their cell. The odor was palpable. During the night, they were bound to their beds. Shit water dripped on their heads.

"That'll show them for breaking the rules." Adams gleefully smiled to herself.

All this was kept from Steve. When he arrived that evening, he was told the three were in therapy. The therapy was to last a week. Steve was not allowed to see the three until the treatment was complete. Steve was not stupid. He knew something was wrong. All attempts at finding the truth were blocked by the staff. Over the years, the employees of the hospital became adept at avoiding relatives and their prying questions. Steve's threats were met with both mental and physical force. When answers weren't coming fast enough, and Steve approached an intern, two guards had to restrain him. He was threatened with a room in the hospital if he didn't settle down.

"Did you see it?" Alex asked as he turned his head to J. D., who was bound in the bed next to him.

"No, you are right, she doesn't have the light like us."

"She sure doesn't," Bernie responded from two beds away.

They talked to each other, but nothing audible was heard. Their silent souls were doing the talking. Souls fueled by the light above their heads.

"I noticed that some of the caretakers' lights are noticeably dimmer by the day. Do you remember Phyllis, the accountant, who would come into our dorm and count the toilet paper rolls in the cabinet next to the toilet? Every week that passed, her light would be a little dimmer. It is as if something bad in her life is slowing diminishing her light," Alex whispered.

"Yeah, maybe she did something bad and God is taking away her light," Bernie said.

"I noticed that our lights never get dimmer. I wonder why?" J. D. asked.

"Maybe it's because we are incapable of sinning anymore. You know, I have not had an impure thought since my mind shut down."

"I have been brain dead since I was an infant and that probably explains why my light is so bright. I really had no chance to sin," Alex retorted.

This spiritual talk went deep into the night. It didn't faze them that their souls were talking to each other. The talk became theologically sophisticated at times. There was discussion of the duality of a human. Man is made up of body and soul. The soul can also be the sum total of human life of the entire person. They discussed the soul in terms of the innermost aspect of man, the most valued part of man, the reflection of God's image, and the essence of life, physical and spiritual. The soul is the spiritual principle in man. Does the soul die with the body? Are the sins of our fathers passed down the generations? Any of the ancient philosophers would have felt at home in this discussion.

The Woodhill Three came to the conclusion that Zelda Adams's soul's light was extinguished because she had done something bad, very bad. Or maybe one of her dead relatives, made of the same mettle, passed down a curse that blackened her soul. Alex, J.D., and Bernie would spend many a night debating the nature of Zelda Adams's soul. If it was within their power, the three would expose Zelda's darkened soul to the world and maybe their world would become a little better. The asylum without Adams would have to be better.

The week of confinement for the three ended on a cruel note. Zelda, wanting to make her mark on the boys, pulled a chair up close to them, lit up a cigarette, and tossed a penny in the air. When she was finished with the cigarette, she put a plug of chew in her mouth and laughed at the three. This mocking hurt the Woodhill Three.

Life for the three became "asylum normal" again. Steve knew he couldn't do anything about the abuse. This was not an enlightened age. No one really cared what happened out at Turney Tech. Steve was not a rich person. To seek legal counsel was out of the question.

The old routine continued. Morning, noon, and night were all the same. The inmates did as they were told. Every time a new therapy was imagined, it was foisted on the patients. The latest was art therapy. If the patient was able to open up his inner artistic being he would somehow get better. The Woodhill Three plus ten other inmates were the first to be exposed to the art therapy. After the first session they had a "talk" about what they learned.

"Do you believe this crap?" J. D. asked.

"I kind of like it," Alex shot back.

"I used to hate art class at St. Ladislas."

The watercolor class turned out to be fun. Alex couldn't even hold a brush. J. D. ate about ten dollars' worth of paint. Bernie shoved the bottle of paint thinner down the front of his pants just because it felt good. To the outside world it was a disaster. For the boys it was like going to an amusement park, all the bright colors and textures and smells. The class that would end the one-week therapy was the spinning pinwheel project.

The hospital hired a young art major, with a minor in psychology, from Western Reserve College. When Sue Alder smiled, it was like the heavens opened and cheer fell to the earth. She handled her assignment the best she could. In the end, her enthusiasm was lost on her pupils. Undaunted, looking always for new ways to reach her charges, she introduced the pinwheel-painting project. The pinwheel project was elemental. A piece of white painting card stock, three feet by three feet, was nailed in the middle of a wooden easel. The easel was attached to a small electric fan motor that would rotate the card stock. The artist would then select whatever color he wanted, and paint, or splatter, colors at the rotating card stock. When the picture was done, Sue hoped to see a rainbow of dashing colors in swirls. If Sue would help each of her artists hold their brushes, the product would resemble art of a sort. Pleased with the outcome of their initial attempts, Sue decided to invite the relatives and staff of her artists to a painting session.

Steve would never pass up a chance to examine a new "therapy." He arrived early and checked on his brother and his friends. Zelda, always nosey and jealous of the staff, also attended. Student after student struggled to make their art come alive. Paint was everywhere. The observers were cautioned to stay far away from the would-be artists and the twirling canvas. The patients were covered in paint. Most of the patients were able to handle the brushes. J. D. and Bernie needed help. When it was Alex's turn, he jumped up and began to paint the rotating canvas, which was completely out of character. Steve, shocked, stood beside his brother, observing him selecting colors and dabbing the paints here and there in what appeared to be random manner. When Alex finished, and as the painting came slowly to a standstill, he, in robotic fashion, returned to his chair and stared into space. A quiet came over the room. The guests, caught off guard, *had trouble comprehending the canvas before them. It was like they had seen a vision of the Virgin Mary.

᯾ ᯾

The roofers would be able to finish repairing the gutters of the main building this beautiful September day in 1872.

"Stan, start the blow torch and get the zinc melted. If we work hard today we could solder all the gutter's seams and be out of here by three o'clock," Jim, the foreman of the job, said in a tone to speed up the work.

"Yeah, maybe we could stop and have a view beers at Kupcik's on the way home." Stan replied in anticipation of a short day, knowing their wives would not be expecting them home until six o'clock.

The two men were at the very top of the tower to the right of the rotunda dome. The blowtorches were lit and placed under the portable

furnaces that resembled the blast furnaces of the steel mills. The sound
of the gas forced through the orifice of the hot tool muffled any more
conversation between the two. The gutters around the pyramid-shaped
tower needed to be soldered and painted once every three years. Stan and
Jim and their crew took a week to build the scaffolding around the top
of each tower. Work on the tower to the left of the rotunda was finished
yesterday. The other crewmembers were breaking down the scaffolding.
The work was to be done today. Each seam in the gutters was inspected
for fissures. Each elbow and coupling joint would need to be soldered.
They were old hands at the job. Like most men of the late-nineteenth
century, they learned their trade from their fathers. The Tinners Red
Company had serviced this building since it was first constructed more
than twenty years ago. The trick to the job was all preparation: build the
scaffold, take all the materials needed up the ladders to their perches,
heat the zinc and irons on the scaffold with the blowtorch furnaces,
solder the seams, paint the inside of each run with Tinners red paint,
check the gutters for leaks the next day, and dismantle the scaffold. They
would draw the water from the eight thousand-gallon storage tanks in
the towers to check for any seams that weren't fastened properly.

It was right before lunch when the repairmen started to solder
the last of the joints on the right tower. They would be done with the
job way before three pm.

"Hand me the iron," Jim shouted over the roar of the torches. Stan carefully reached over, holding the scaffolding for good measure, and handed Jim the white-hot iron. Jim, holding the gutter with his right hand, reached over and grabbed the iron.

"Finished," Jim shouted to Stan. "Turn off the torches and let's go have a few cold ones."

Surprisingly, it was Joseph Turney, a Newburgh trustee, who first saw the smoke from his house in Newburgh. He was first to notify the Cleveland Fire Department. By the time anyone realized what was happening, the fire had engulfed the main building of the asylum and created chaos. The inmates all but panicked. The escaping patients filled the surrounding neighborhood, scaring the locals. Six people died that day in the inferno, including Mary Walker, a seamstress at the asylum.

Mary, a beloved member of the staff, was trapped in the flames. She was at the door of a stairwell when debris from the fire took away her only escape. The stairs leading to safety were ripped from their casing right in front of her. The flames behind Mary and under her made it evident that there was no escape. Shouts from below, imploring her to jump, were to no avail. Mary wanted to jump, but her feet seemed to be held fast. She was terrified. The crowd below watched as she was burned alive.

Steve, the art teacher, and others could not believe what Alex had painted. What they saw in the swirled painting was an extremely well-wrought picture of *two* women fighting for their lives in a doorway. The women were paired one in front of the other. The woman behind was holding tightly on to the one in front. Her facial expression was one of glee. The time for revenge was now. She knew she had only seconds to either free Mary's foot or escape and save herself. The art class recognized only one of the women. Other than the length of the hair, the woman holding Mary back looked strangely like Zelda Adams. Zelda, startled to the core, knew the woman.

The story of the awful fire was front-page news that September 1872. The six who'd died were Benjamin Burgess, Isaac Hearn, William Edwards, Alfred Brown, Edward Morgan, and Mary Walker.

There was no mention of another woman. Our art aficionados, if they were to name this apparition, would only have to ask Zelda.

Armensha Adams was Zelda's grandmother.

The Woodhill Three glanced at each other, as if to say, that explains everything.

The glow of light from the Woodhill Three was blinding.

"Where's the painting?" Dr. Andrisek, looking at an exhausted Steve, inquired.

"Zelda grasped the painting with both hands and slowly walked out of the room, smirking all the way," Steve replied.

"I guess she is not done with her mischief," added Drabik, the lawyer.

"A great many medical journals document strange occurrences dealing with autistic children. They have extraordinary powers at times," the doctor continued.

"Did the young art teacher react to the painting?" John asked.

"Yes, and I doubt she will return. Her face turned an off color, and she ran after Zelda," Steve answered.

A discussion about the human brain followed. Joel, Karol, and Charlie couldn't grasp the idea that Alex had been able to penetrate the past and paint a picture of it. They thought Steve made this all up to get the attention of the group. He would to anything to get back at Zelda. At the very least, they thought the art teacher had painted the piece beforehand and had somehow switched the work. The discussion broke down into a religious argument about God giving certain people "powers." The children of Fatima had the power to see the Virgin Mary. St. Francis had the ability to talk to animals. Karol, the only Protestant of the group, would have nothing of the so-called miracles of the Catholic church. He said after the New Testament ended all miracles ended. Jesus interrupted the natural course of things to prove his divinity, and that was that, end of story, no more miracles. Charlie said God could do anything he wanted. He could even change the Bible if he chose to. Joel said if God is a good God and can do everything why does he allow pain and suffering in this his world? John interrupted saying these are all mysteries of the Holy Faith and we are not supposed to know God's thoughts and reasons. Charlie continued that we all have free will and we sin and that is why we have pain and suffering. We all deserve to have pain and die. Doc and the lawyer, ignoring the others, were in the back by the paint mixer talking. They decided to visit Steve's brother and talk to this Zelda person. They wanted to see for themselves what had transpired.

As things happen, Dr. Andrisek and counselor Drabik did not visit Steve's brother. Zelda burned Alex's artwork and died soon after. The art teacher never returned to work. Alex never showed his artistic side again. The Woodhill Three died one by one. Alex was the last. On his deathbed he was said to be drawing imaginary pictures in the air.

Chapter 9
THE TRAINS

"John, why don't you sell electric trains in your store?"

"Semen hardware sells toys. I sell hardware. Trains are for kids."

Karol thought all hardware stores sold electric trains. He remembered visiting New York City where a store called Madison Hardware exclusively sold Lionel trains. Not one item of hardware was to be found in that store. They had trains stacked to the ceiling. Even the Lionel Corporation came to Madison for parts for their discontinued lines.

November always brought the model train enthusiasts out. The Christmas season of 1956 was no exception. Talk in the store would be about who made the best model trains. According to most of the back-store group, Lionel was the leader. Yes, some could argue that American Flyer was superior, especially their S gauge line. There was always one guy who would favor Marx trains. Marx trains were cheaply made, litho on tin, and no one would ever compare them to Lionel.

"The Lionel scale model Hudson was the best pre-war scale locomotive ever made," Karol said.

The Hudson first came out in 1939. It weighed a model ton and was huge. The detail of trucks (wheels), shiny nickel pull rods, headlight, and whistle made it the most sought after model locomotive ever. Just imagine Christmas morning, with this ozone-leaking electric behemoth with its long assortment of cars following, circling the Christmas tree. Heaven on earth for any male young or old. Most kids of the 1950s owned at least one electric train set. The lucky ones had Lionel.

Hans, a German and Lutheran friend of Karol, would often join in on the discussions at Mader Hardware. He was a young immigrant from the Prussia Schrofhiede Forest area, north of Berlin. Ask Hans what he thought was the best model trains made; he said the German made Marklin. Marklin made great model trains before the war. Europe's Lionel equivalent. Wartime production preempted civilian industry. Marklin ceased war production of model trains. Like all older men stuck in their childhood past, the train argument turned heated and only settled down when Hans let it be known that he had a train story.

The adventure began when Albert was twelve years old in 1943. Albert's family vacationed at their cottage in the Dollnsees Lake area about eighty miles north of Berlin. The Prussian Schorfheide Forest surrounded the Big Dollnsees. The Strauss families vacationed there since the turn of the century. The "cottage" was a three thousand-square-foot structure that could easily house two families. Robert Strauss was a lawyer in Berlin who used the cottage as an escape from the tension of the time. He would always invite his partner and his family to vacation with him. Richard Roth and his wife, Beta, had one child named Hilda. Hilda was eleven years old and precocious. Albert and Hilda were inseparable. Their favorite pastime was exploring the woods and catching butterflies. Linda Strauss would always warn the children not to venture far. The forest could be dangerous. It was a favorite hunting ground for the rich of the big cities. If a bear didn't get you, a stray bullet might.

"Hilda, let's go and catch butterflies."

Albert didn't need to say anything more. Off they went into the fields. A well-worn path would lead the way. Albert was tall for his age and towered over Hilda. She would look up to him and felt secure. Hilda was a blonde-haired, blue-eyed baby. Albert's hair was white and his eyes were the dark blue of the ocean. The two could easily pass for brother and sister. Their parents would say half seriously that the children should someday marry.

Butterflies were Albert's preoccupation. He knew the Latin names of all the varieties of the region. Hilda did too and could even spell them. What Albert liked, Hilda loved. It wasn't long before the two had a collection of more than fifty butterflies. Sometimes the collecting would force the two deep into the forest. In the woods' open areas the butterflies flourished.

One day, at the end of June, Albert and Hilda decided to add to their butterfly collection. They took a jar and net. Only one net was needed because Albert was always the one to catch the insects. Hilda held the jar and was ready to open it and close it on command. Too far into the woods and no butterflies to be found, they realized they had to turn around. Hilda was having too much fun and begged Albert to keep going.

"Only a little while longer," Albert said.

The two stopped to rest under an oak tree, sitting amongst the leaves and acorns. Albert was reviewing the catch of the day when he realized Hilda had fallen asleep. His first thought was to wake her but when he spotted a bright red butterfly, the chase was on. He ran to the meadow below and chased the brightly colored insect into the woods. He ran up to a giant tree and rested his back on it. He heard a noise and turned to run and was catapulted into the air, falling into a heap on the ground. He was stunned but managed to look up.

A large, fat man dressed in multicolored clothing hung over him. The man put down his hunting rifle, laughed, and offered his hand to the boy. Albert realized he had bounced off the stranger's belly. Albert began to laugh too. The noise of laughter woke Hilda and she came running to see the stranger and Albert talking. In all the times they had gone into the woods, the two had never seen another person, let alone one so large and colorful.

The big man went out of his way to be kind and gentle with the kids. He asked them their names and where they came from. Albert cautiously told him the minimum. He told him they were on vacation with their families, and they were sorry if they were on his land. He laughed and said no one can own a forest and they were perfectly welcomed here. He did caution that about two miles down the road, just over the ridge, was a construction crew adding on to his cottage. He really didn't want them to disturb the men and suggested the construction site could be a danger to them. He gave each of them a piece of chocolate and wished them well.

As the man disappeared over the ridge, Albert and Hilda exchanged looks, and they knew they just had to explore the fat man's cottage. Forbid children something and look out. It was late and two miles was a long way to trek back. Planning was needed to go on this forbidden trek. It would have to wait for another day. Following the path home, they planned the exploration in the greatest of detail, details only a twelve and eleven-year- old could imagine.

ཆ◎ ◎ན

The planning took longer than the children expected. They knew two miles was a long way and would take a long time to hike. They gathered up what they thought was important for the trip. Walking sticks were a must; the adults always had them when they went to the forest. Hilda chimed she couldn't go anywhere for such a long time without her Wolfy, a stuffed dog. Albert knew it would be futile to deny her Wolfy. He was more practical and said they would have to take some water and sandwiches. They decided together that each could take one of their lucky stones and a bag of candy. Hilda thought of an ax and matches to build a fire. Albert reminded Hilda that they were strictly forbidden to play with matches. He was good at thinking ahead. Their mothers and fathers would not know of their adventure. They decided to leave on Saturday morning; the day the parents go to visit friends. Albert knew that they would be gone the whole day and their nanny would immediately fall asleep.

They had a false start when the nanny didn't fall asleep until late morning. The sun was high in the sky and it was a great day for a hike in the woods. Albert thought that he ought to mark the path as they went along. He was in charge and didn't want to get lost. He knew all the fairy tales so he crossed off leaving a trail of bread. Hilda suggested they use their candy, but upon thinking that suggestion over they realized that their stomachs said no. Always resourceful, Albert decided on paint. Hilda jumped with glee and begged to be the one to strike the path with paint. Hilda took one little jar of watercolor paint and a small brush. The plan was complete and off they skipped down the path to the forest, Hilda painting the way. Albert laughed but let her do the important job with one warning: "Don't run out of paint." No sooner had the last word come out of Albert's mouth when Hilda reported the paint was gone.

Hilda was first to notice something was wrong. She found one of her trail marks. They seemed to be going in circles. Albert, a little embarrassed, said they should try again. They weren't tired but they were hungry. The sandwich meat was a little slimy for Hilda so she didn't eat. In a clearing, they found some ripe berries. The berries glistened in the sun like cats' eyes. Hilda ate until her tummy was full, and then they set out in a different direction. They lost their original path.

Albert pushed the undergrowth ahead of Hilda. The patches of briars appeared more often and deeper than before. The briars whipped across their faces. Hilda got hit a good one and started to cry and blood was oozing from her face. Albert said it was just a scratch and said she was a big girl and should stop crying. Ignoring him, she cried louder. Albert couldn't quiet her and finally thought of the candy. She took the bait and ate all of it.

Albert estimated that they had been hiking for about one hour. Hilda kept asking him if they were there yet. She said Wolfy was getting tired. Hilda gave Wolfy to Albert. Wolfy smelled of dry milk and vomit and he gave the stuffed animal back with a laugh.

"You wanted to bring Wolfy, now you have to take care of him."

"No I didn't. You told me to take him," she cried with not one ounce of truth.

"No I didn't."

"Yes you did."

"No."

"Yes."

"No a thousand times plus the last number."

Albert knew he would get nowhere with her. She was spoiled and always got her own way. He took the stuffed animal and said under his breath, "Girls are a pain!"

"You are mean and I hate you."

"Ah, shut up."

No trail to follow, our little travelers went in what they thought was a straight line down to a ravine. At the bottom of the ravine was a rivulet. Hilda shook, looked down, and said, "No way!." Albert didn't care and jumped to the first boulder on a ledge going down. He turned to call Hilda, but she was gone. He knew he couldn't crawl back up. Down he went. The whole adventure would last about two scraped knees and one hurt toe. Finally at the rivulet, he took his shoe off and soaked his hurt toe in the cool water.

Hilda, sitting on a big rock across the flowing water, was laughing. Albert again was beaten by this imp. Joining her on the rock, Albert asked how she got there so fast.

"Down the steps a little ways down," was all she said, smirking.

Albert said he hated her.

"So?"

"So nothing."

A butterfly landed nearby and off the two went. They ran and ran only as little kids do. They didn't pay attention to where they were. Into and out of a clearing they ran. Back to the little river four times. They didn't have a net and soon found out how hard it was to catch a butterfly. Exhausted, they sat down by a patch of daisies.

Forgetting about their hatred for one another, they realized they were far away from their home and lost. Hilda rested her head on Albert's shoulder and began to cry. Then a loud sound of rifle fire was heard in the distance. Hoping it was the big fat man hunting again, they ran to the noise.

Before they got to the sound, they saw a huge sign saying, "Danger beyond this point. All trespassers will be arrested." Not knowing what "trespassers" meant, they threw rocks at the sign and giggled as they hit their marks. As they were about to head forward, ignoring the sign, a man stepped out from behind a tree.

"Where are you two going and why are you trespassing on government land?" asked a scowling, huge man in funny clothes and hat. There was that word again: "trespassing." They both turned in fear and couldn't answer a question they couldn't understand. Trembling, they soon realized they were in deep trouble. Albert asked the man what "trespassing" meant.

"Listen, you little snot. I don't need any lip from you. Answer me or I will shoot you on the spot." He put his hand on his holster. "Where are your parents?"

More men showed themselves from behind the trees. That's when it hit Albert; these were soldiers. The funny hats were helmets. The same reality hit Hilda. She peed her pants.

The soldier grabbed the children, threw them over his shoulder, and placed them into the back of a truck. The soldiers talked amongst themselves, and after a few minutes, the truck started up and they were to experience the bumpiest ride of their lives.

Hilda threw up her berries. *Great*, Albert thought. *Now she is covered in berries and pee.* He thought maybe they shouldn't have started this adventure. Before he put into words what he thought, the truck came to a sudden stop. A soldier opened the back of the truck and ordered the children out. They took one look around and then looked at each other and got scared again. They were in a yard that had statues all over the place. A buck was sitting on a pedestal of concrete guarding the front door of a massive building. In the yard was a statue of a naked warrior. Hilda and Albert didn't much like it and blushed again and said "yucky."

Servants, all dressed in white like nurses, took over from the soldiers and ushered them into the front door.

Albert and Hilda started to tremble again when they looked at all the deer horns hanging between full-length rugs. The rugs depicted hunting scenes. Off to one side on the floor lay a huge bear rug. The bear had his mouth opened showing his ghastly teeth.

"I want to go home," Hilda screamed.

They soon learned they couldn't leave because one of the servants locked the entrance door. Albert tried to comfort Hilda but it was no used.

"Are you a nurse?" Albert asked one of the three women.

"Heavens no!" she responded. "We are housekeepers." One of the servants asked Hilda what had happened to her dress. Hilda told her about the berries and the bumpy ride in the truck. The owner's daughter was her size and before Hilda knew it she was dressed in new beautiful clothes. The children didn't know the owner's name. He was just the fat man who owned this cottage. They knew instinctively not to say those words out loud. The servants returned to their quarters on a cautionary note warning the children to sit down and don't touch anything.

As soon as the housekeepers left, Albert and Hilda got up and walked around the vast hall. They inspected the bear rug, making sure the bear was really dead. Assuring themselves that the bear was not capable of hurting them, they jumped on the pelt. They wrestled with the skin, dragging it all around the hall. Albert was the horse, the bear was the wagon, and Hilda was Heidi out for a ride.

At the far end they spotted a full figure of armor. They skipped down the hall. Albert told Hilda there was a dead knight inside the armor. Hilda froze and became scared again. Albert said he was kidding and they should play hide and seek. Albert was to hide first.

He found a spot behind a statue of a big naked man holding a spear. He knew Hilda would never find him there. Finished counting, Hilda, avoiding the knight in armor, went looking for Albert. She looked down the hall and began to slowly walk down the center. Forgetting about the game, she began to dance and twirl. She imagined herself a princess. Albert came out from hiding and said, "Ah, come on. I thought you wanted to play hide and seek." Just as he was finishing his question, in came the big fat man.

The children ran to him, remembering how nice he was.

"Well, my little ones, you managed to find my hideout. Are you hungry?"

He pressed a button on the wall behind him and a servant in white appeared.

"Please get my little ones something to eat."

Within minutes the children were sitting at a thirty-place dining room table right off the hall. The big fat man asked how their parents were and if they were going to visit him soon. They were interrupted when the servant came with a platter full of cold cuts and bread. Hilda's eyes lit up when another servant came in with a chocolate cake.

"You must tell your mothers and fathers to come to my party next weekend. We are going to have a wild game roast." The big fat man wrote out two invitations.

"How much time do you little ones have for this visit?"

Hilda frowned, but Albert said about two hours.

"But really much less because we have to walk all the way back."

The big fat man said not to worry about the time; he would take care of it. "Follow me and I will show you something we can play." He took them down the hall past the knight in armor. Hilda made a wide circle around it. The fat man smiled at her route.

"She's scared," Albert said with a tone of superiority.

"Well, she should be. That dead knight comes alive once a month, and I think tonight's the night."

Hilda ran toward the door. Albert told her to stop being scared and grow up. They passed through another room. The fat man put his finger to his lips, and all was solemn and quiet. He pointed out a small shrine to his dead wife in the corner of the room. He guided them to the shrine and spoke in a low, prayerful voice.

"This is my love. She has been gone for more than ten years."

"Where did she go?" Hilda asked.

"To heaven."

The shrine was about five feet wide by six feet tall. A picture of the man's wife was hanging in the middle of the altar. Two candles, that showed use, were on either side of the picture. A tapestry depicting the Holy Family was draped the bottom. The shrine was encased in a red and gold velvet shroud. A kneeler was to one side. A tear came to the fat man's eye and the children began to understand and wiped their eyes. He motioned them away and up some stairs leading to what turned out to be the attic.

When they reached the attic door, the fat man opened it and the room was pitch black. He told them to hold hands and slowly follow him. The children could not guess what was in the attic. The man went about halfway into the room when he came to a sudden stop. He told the children to stare straight ahead.

With a flick of a switch, the room lit up, showing a huge layout of model trains. The trains were running in all directions on the floor of the attic. The engines' headlights showing the engineer the road ahead. When they told the story in years to come, they talked about hundreds of feet of track, whole villages of people, country scenes of farms, steel mills in a city, and an airport with military planes that flew over the layout dropping bombs on the trains and factories.

After the war, when the children were grown, they learned that the model train set consisted of 321 feet of electric train tracks with tunnels, bridges and many fighter bomber airplanes. The value of the train set was $265,000.

The fat man said, "Children, do you want to play trains with me?"

They jumped for joy. He showed them how to run the controls on the transformers. They raced the trains down the tracks. They were unaware of scale speed. The big fat man encouraged them to race the engines and when they would crash and fall off the tracks, he laughed as hard as the kids. They played the game of how many trains each could bomb. Albert hit more than Hilda. The fat man hit the most. He had more practice at destruction. They played and played and lost track of time.

A manservant dressed in high riding boots came into the attic and announced that a forest ranger came to the door of the cottage enquiring about two lost children. He said the parents of the children were out of their minds with worry.

"Tell the ranger that the children will be returned home immediately. Get my car!" the fat man ordered.

Of course, the children were disappointed. They wanted to play more. They pleaded with their host to no avail. The man gave them one last chance at the bombing and off they went home. The fat man stopped to whisper something to the servant. He said yes and they all started down the stairs.

The trip home took a very short time. The children never saw such a wonderful automobile. It was a convertible. The fat man told the driver to go as fast as he can. This time Hilda didn't pee. She just sat back and let the wind blow in her hair. Albert said he would someday own a car just like this.

They arrived home to be greeted by their parents. The mothers ran to the car to hug the found children. The children leaped from the car to the embrace of their mothers. When the big fat man exited the auto, the whole mood changed. The fathers immediately stood at attention and everyone quieted down. Years later, when they would tell this story, they would recall how serious their parents became and how they groveled to the fat man and couldn't thank him enough for finding their children.

The Buick started to speed away when it suddenly stop and drove in reverse. The fat man waved to the children to come to the car. Reaching out the window, he gave them each a wrapped present. The children ran to their parents and asked if they could open them right away.

"Yes, of course." They opened packages revealed two brand new electric train engines and tenders embossed with the letters HG.

∽ ∾

That was the end of Hans's story. The group in the store worried over the initials HG. Hans told the group that he had a letter to read to them that would explain everything.

Hans began to read:

August 2, 1944

Carin Hall, Germany

Dear Albert and Hilda,

I hope you enjoy playing with the engines I gave you. We had such a good time playing trains I wished that our time together would never end. As you probably know by now, I am a very busy man, but if you come for vacation next year, please come and see me so we can play trains again. Have a good year in school.

Your best friend,

Heil Hitler!

Reich Marshal Hermann Göring

Hans carefully put the letter down and looked up at the inquiring faces of the group. Hans then revealed a package containing two prewar Marklin German-made electric train engines. "My full name is Albert Hans Strauss; my wife, Hilda, calls me Albert."

Hermann Göring. How could such a man, a murderer, a degenerate, find joy in playing trains with kids? Göring, Hitler's Reich marshal. Göring, the builder of the gas chambers. Göring, the thief who stole precious art from those he killed. Göring, the egomaniac. Göring the family man who had killed scores of innocent children. This madman who could find pleasure in killing and playing trains at the same time.

These were the thoughts of the men in the hardware store some ten years after the end of the war.

"Hans—or should I call you Albert?—you must explain to us how such a bad man could have this mild mannered about himself," John said.

"As Jesus said, even our enemies are gentle to their families," Steve interjected.

The question of good and bad residing in one man perplexed the gathering. The whiskey bottle was passed around and an argument about the nature of God and man started when Joel asked, "Is man basically good or basically bad?" How could an all-good God have created such an ugly, despicable man?

"That's easy. The Bible said there is none righteous; not even one," Charlie said.

"If everyone has a bad streak in them and God created such a creature, isn't it God's problem? God has no problems. Oh, yeah!

How about pain? Would an all-loving God allow his children to suffer pain, let's say the pain of dying from cancer? God, in the person of Jesus, only suffered three hours on the cross when, for instance, it could take years to die of cancer. What's fair about that? And don't give me 'it's God's will' bullshit." How could a good God knowingly inflict that kind of death on anyone? That kind of God is a sadist."

The shop whistle blew and the men continued to fight as they left for work. Nothing was resolved. Joel did say he wanted to tell a story about a priest he once knew. The story had to wait until Saturday after work. Sometimes the group would meet late and continue the discussion with the help of a bottle. This was special. Steve was celebrating his birthday. By the time the store was closed, the men were crowded in the back awaiting Joel's story.

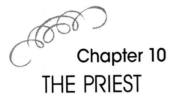

Chapter 10
THE PRIEST

Jerry knew he had to go to confession. He'd sinned, and First Friday was this week. As he walked to the church he examined his conscience as only a twelve-year-old could. It was a short examination. The sins, such as lying to his father, would be easy to confess, but the sins that his catechism lumped together as "impure" bothered him all week. How do you tell the priest that you had impure thoughts and did impure acts? He was stuck. This was the first time since his first confession at age seven that he had to confess his impurities. What would the priest say to a boy who thought he was the only one in the whole world who did such things? Would he get angry and not forgive him his sins? Does he know the sound of his voice? Would he put his face to the voice? If he didn't confess his sins, he could not go to communion. God gave the Catholic Church the right to make laws. This was one of its laws. Break it and go to hell.

Jerry knew what he had to do. The closer he got to church the more nervous he became. His hands began to sweat, and he trembled as he walked. He saw other children from his class. They were going to confession too, but they were laughing and goofing around. Jerry thought, *How can they be so happy knowing they are going to confession? See? I must be the only one who has sins of impurity to confess.*

The church sat at the summit of Lamontier hill and could be viewed from as far away as downtown Cleveland. When he got to the church, he entered through the side door. The church was built for a large congregation. Old Father Mark, the original pastor, wanted it to service the growing population of newly arrived immigrants. So he built big. The inside of the church was a huge domed covered space. The main altar looked like a smaller version of the Vatican. Four pillars held up a canopy some forty feet high above the altar. A mural depicting saints and angels climbing up to heaven climbed the wall behind the altar. Four side altars, used only on special occasions, lined the interior. Four confessionals were conveniently located at the side entrances.

Jerry lined up behind a row of his classmates. He was about to go into the confessional when Janet came up behind him and held him back. She whispered, "It's not your turn yet." In his nervousness, he'd lost track of who was next. Janet was the prettiest girl in his class. He turned and glanced at her but said nothing, his face telling everything. He knew for sure she had never had an impure thought or had done a bad deed.

It was his turn, and he quickly entered the confessional. He said what he'd been taught. "Bless me, Father, for I have sinned ..." He quickly went through the easy-to-confess sins and mumbled about his impurities. Father James stopped him cold and asked him to repeat what he'd said. With much effort, he did. Father James quickly absolved him of his sins, and Jerry was out the door. It was so easy he wondered why he'd fretted about it. He hurried out of the church with a light heart. He was free. No hell for him.

He managed to be chaste one day. He'd thought about Janet a lot since his confession. He thought about her but not in a pure way. He'd never seen a naked girl, except when his father took him to the auto mechanic's garage. There on the back wall of the shop hung various pin-ups in different stages of undress. His father told him not to look at the pictures. That command didn't stop him from sneaking a peek. The girls all looked happy. Jerry wandered why the pictures only showed their tops and butts but never their fronts down below. The good part. He knew if he stared too long at the images, he would have to perform an impure act.

He remembered what Sister Mary Angelus said: "Jesus will never give you a temptation that you can't overcome with willpower." He wrestled with the temptation all day long. He thought pure thoughts all day long. He said a hundred Hail Mary's, fifty Our Fathers, and two hundred Glory Bes. After gym he took a cold shower. Jerry did the impure act that night. No holy communion for him. He was lost again. Confession next Friday or hell.

⁓∾ ∾⁓

Father James's parents died in the flu epidemic of 1918. James, then twelve years old, was taken to an orphanage run by the Sisters of Notre Dame. James's given name was John. He was a strong, healthy baby. As he got older, the good sisters realized John was very bright. Once every school term the bishop would visit the orphanage and talk to the mother superior about prospects for the seminary. John's name came up and mother superior was told to act. John, now age fourteen, became a special interest to the nuns. They became concerned about all aspects of John's life. He became a good Catholic boy.

Sister Mary Angelus was a good nun. She performed her holy duties to perfection. Whenever anything had to get done, whether at the orphanage's church or in the school, she was the first to volunteer. Sister Angelus was the glue that kept the orphanage together. She loved God above all others. She loved the ritual, the ceremony and traditions of the Church. She loved teaching and especially loved the children. Parents went to Sister Angelus if there was a problem at school. John would seek sister's advice even after he graduated from elementary school. Sister always made time for John.

Jerry became hypervigilant about his faith. He felt that he could not be too good. He now went to confession once a week and communion every day. There were no little sins to Jerry. All sin would earn him hell. He developed a perfect Catholic conscience based on guilt. He said his daily prayers and if he missed a prayer time he would pray twice as much the next day. At sixteen, he no longer committed impure thoughts or acts. He totally suppressed all sexual feelings. If he did slip, he ran to confession. Absolution was easy. He became a server at Mass. He took serving Mass very seriously and was the first one at church. He would lay out the vestments for the priest. He would make sure the water and wine cruets were placed correctly at the side of the altar. When father arrived he would help him put on his vestments. After Mass, he'd make sure that everything was put away properly. Sometimes he would go up on the pulpit and pretend to give a sermon. The view from the pulpit, way above the congregation, made him feel important. He wanted to become a priest. His fellow servers thought he was weird.

Under the guidance and love of Sister Angelus, John became James, a priest. It was quite an easy transformation from Catholic orphan to priest. The strict religious environment of the orphanage became the strict religious environment of the seminary. He was used to the regimen and thrived on it. Sister Angelus went to his ordination and told him he would make a good priest. Father James was assigned as an assistant pastor of Our Lady of Fatima diocesan church. Above all, Father James was a good and holy man—Chaucer's parson.

Father James made friends easily.

Jerry was more than interested in the priesthood, he made up his mind that he would be a priest. He would do anything for Father James. Problems arose at school between Jerry and Alec, a fellow student. Alec was prone to boast about dates with girlfriends and loved to tell all the intimate details of his petting sessions at the picture shows.

"I don't want to hear about your dates and petting."

"Ah, come on and loosen up. Live a little. Life is too short."

"If you don't stop I am going to tell Father James on you."

"What are you guys fighting about now?" Father James asked.

"Nothing, Father," Alec said.

"If it is nothing, why is Jerry so red in the face?"

"It's just Alec telling his silly stories about girls."

Changing the subject, Jerry told Father James that he'd arranged everything for tomorrow's wedding at Our Lady of Fatima.

"Isn't that Sister Angelus's job?" Father asked in a not-so-pleasing way. The truth was Father was a little tired of Jerry's overzealous behavior. Jerry would sign up for all different server assignments: funerals, weddings, novenas, and he never shied away from 5:30 a.m. Mass (most normal young men hated getting up so early).

"I thought sister needed a little break from her routine."

"Don't do things on your own. You must ask first before you go into the sanctuary. Do you understand?"

"Yes, Father."

Jerry understood, but he didn't like it.

Jerry couldn't wait for recess this Monday morning. He opened his desk and got his missal and ran to the church. He made it just in time; a funeral had ended and the church would be deserted for the rest of the morning. He sat in the first pew. He opened his missal and began looking for the prayers that would be said this week. Wednesday was Ash Wednesday. He loved Lent, and he wanted to be completely prepared. As he was thumbing through the pages of the missal he looked up and noticed that the tabernacle door of the main altar was partially opened. He looked around to see if anyone else was in the church, and when he was satisfied that he was the only one, he slowly raised himself off the kneeler and walked up the steps to the communion railing. Looking around the church again he removed the chain and cross from entrance to the sanctuary. He got as far as the stairs going up to the high altar when he heard Sister Angelus talking to another nun about the preparations for Lent. It was too late for him to hide.

"Why are you in the sanctuary? Who gave you permission to remove the chain and approach the altar?"

"I'm sorry, Sister."

"Well, I am going to tell Father James about this."

As they left the church together, Jerry looked over his shoulder at the main altar.

Funerals were always the most fun to serve, or at least Jerry saw it that way. You are excused from class and you get to ride in a big black Cadillac to the cemetery. The Mass was minor-key dreary. At the cemetery, he was always disappointed when they left without seeing the casket lowered into the ground. When he becomes bishop that would be one of the first things changed. After the service in the cemetery, brunch was served.

Jerry was fascinated with the deceased. He never understood how dead people could look so good. Their makeup and hair always looked perfect. The dead person was dressed in his or her best clothes.

The wreath above the casket was always beautiful and expensive. The flowers around the casket gave off their natural aroma. A new rosary in hand and a crucifix in the middle of the casket finished the scene. He loved how solemn everyone was at the funeral home, but he knew he could never grieve like the families. He thought it strange the way they carried on. Even if his mother died, he couldn't cry like they did.

Jerry knew he had to practice this funeral business. He was going to be a priest, and he needed to know all the procedures. He saw nothing wrong or morbid about practicing funerals. He needed a dead body to practice the funeral ritual. He had no siblings so he couldn't practice on them. If he had a sister he could borrow one of her dolls for the ceremony. Jerry had a secret. He like to kill things. Ants and spiders were his favorite victims.

"A dead ant or a spider can hardly take the place of a cadaver. I need a larger animal, like a cat or squirrel. The neighbor's cat would be the ideal subject for my funeral. There he is now just walking all proud across my backyard. I need to plan this just right. The cat has to die."

Jerry lured the cat with a can of sardines. When the cat got close enough, Jerry grabbed him by its hind legs, held him up, and struck him hard on the back of his head and killed him. He debated whether to gut the cat or not. After a little thought, he decided to keep the cat, guts and all. Jerry found a cardboard box and placed the cat in it. He took the box to his room, which would serve as a funeral home. Father Gerald (as he called himself) greeted the imaginary family and friends. He said a rosary for the cat's soul and reminded everyone that the funeral Mass would take place two days later in the church in the basement of his house. Seeing that the cat was starting to smell, he moved the funeral up a day. The deceased's name was Mr. Robert Sliver.

Mr. Sliver began to rot pretty fast. Jerry's mother sent Jerry to the basement to see if a rat was caught in a trap. Jerry knew where the odor was coming from and made immediate arrangements for burial. He got one of his father's raincoats for a vestment. He took some of his mother's candles that she used for electric outages for the altar. Chairs were set up for his imaginary relatives and friends.

Jerry reached into his pocket and pulled out about ten consecrated hosts he had taken from the altar the day before. After all, he wanted the funeral to be real. It was his good luck that the tabernacle was open the other day. Who would notice a few missing hosts? Jerry started the requiem in not-so-perfect Latin. He went through the whole ritual of the Requiem Mass. One thing for sure was the cat had a good Catholic send off.

Mr. Sliver was buried in Jerry's backyard under a wooden cross.

Jerry went to school with a happy heart. He was proud of himself for the funeral service he'd performed. His happy-heart feeling was short-lived. When he got to his classroom, Sister Angelus told him Father James wanted to see him immediately at the rectory.

"Father, did you want to see me?"

"Yes, come in to my office. Sister told me she caught you in the sanctuary yesterday."

"Father, I was making sure the altar was cleared after the funeral."

"Didn't I tell you not to do that, that Sister would do it? You disobeyed me again."

"I am sorry, Father."

"Also, I'm missing ten consecrated hosts. I put twenty Eucharists in the chalice for the funeral. Five people took communion at the funeral, fifteen were left in the chalice, and now there are only five left. You know only a priest may touch the consecrated hosts. This is a grievous sin. Did you take the hosts?"

After being caught at the altar, he couldn't very well deny he'd taken the hosts. He had five left. He slowly pulled them out of his pants pocket.

Father took them and they went into the church to return them to the tabernacle. Father James said a prayer and replaced them into the tabernacle. Father told Jerry he would have to take two swats on his behind and stay after school for a week and write an essay on the Eucharist. From that day on Jerry hated Father James. He wished Father was the size of a cat so he could kill him just like he did Mr. Sliver.

April 29 was to be one of the most important days for Our Lady of Fatima Parish. It was a day that was marked by the arrival of Cardinal Olaksky, an escaped prelate from behind the iron curtain, and his land, Slovakia. Everyone in the parish school would have a role to play in the ceremonies. The choir would practice three nights a week, the nuns would prepare the altar with newly cut flowers, and all the grades would march in the processional. Father James also wanted Sister Angelus to pick five of her best students to welcome the Cardinal. Jerry was one of the selected.

Each student was to compose a three-minute piece to welcome the cardinal. Father made the five come to the abbey to practice in front of him. The recitations were all poorly written; even Jerry's needed work.

Father James decided he would have to work one-on-one with each student. He set up a schedule for the meetings in the evening at the parish house. Jerry was the last to see Father. It was Friday night when he walked up the long sidewalk up to the rear of the rectory. The daffodils were just starting to blossom after what could be called one of the wettest springs on recorded. Rain clouds were forming. More rain tonight.

When he got to the door of the rectory, he rang the doorbell and an old lady answered. Her name was Rosa, and she was Jerry's *teta*—his aunt. She was surprised to see her nephew at the back door.

"Well, if it isn't my nephew Jerry. What brings you to the parish house?"

"Hello, Teta Rosa. I came to see Father James about my greeting for the cardinal."

"Well, you came to the right place. I'm just finishing up the supper dishes. I will go call him."

Teta Rosa left the room long enough for Jerry to look around. He went into the kitchen and saw the priest had had chicken for supper. Jerry was a bit surprised; he never gave it a thought that priests actually ate. Rosa came back and told Jerry Father James was waiting for him in the parlor. Rosa escorted him down a long hallway with walls made of deep, rich mahogany. He was never in the rectory before, so this was all new to him. The décor reeked of a manly presence. There was pipe smoke in the air. Jerry didn't know Father smoked a pipe. He was shown to the library. Books were everywhere: stacked on the floor, shelves up to the ceiling. Books of all kinds—not just religious. He guessed there were many things he didn't know of the daily living of a priest.

When Jerry entered, he saw Father James across the room, smoking his pipe and reading his breviary, the prayers of the hours. Jerry first thoughts were he didn't want to be here. His dislike for father was palpable.

"Jerry, is there anything wrong? You look sullen."

"No, I'm all right."

No, he was not all right. Jerry decided Father was his enemy. Everything Father James said to him was filtered through what had become his demented mind. Father reminded Jerry that he owed him two swats. He called Teta Rosa to the library to act as a witness. Rosa was not aware of what Jerry had done to deserve the swats. She knew if Father said he deserved him, then he deserved them. Jerry took the swats without complaining. The rest of the evening was devoted to the recitation. Jerry's speech turned out to be the best of the five.

Over the years Father James became friends with many families throughout the diocese. It was not uncommon for him to visit and have supper at parishioners' homes as many as three times a week. After Mass on Sundays, he would volunteer at soup kitchens throughout the city. He visited nursing homes well into his eighties. But, above all, he would not miss a chance to be around children. He took groups of kids to amusement parks all around the state. He loved to take them to the movies and buy them candy and popcorn. Father lived for the happiness of young children.

His parishioners of Our Lady of Fatima would plead with him to slow down. He would tell them he would have plenty of time to rest in heaven. Now was the time to live. When he turned eighty, his close friends made him the object of an intervention. They sat him down and told him he has to stop all this running around and retire from the priesthood. He could go into a nice rest home and live peacefully until the Lord takes him.

Father James listened to all their concerns and promised he would weigh what they said. When they left, he got on the computer and ordered one hundred tickets to Cedar Point for the weekend. He knew his friends meant him well, but he just couldn't stop. He was going to take the kids in his parish to the amusement park. He thought, *And this is not going to be the last time, like in the story books. I will greet the next decade like in the story books. I will greet the next decade of my life doing what I like most—being a priest and having fun.* Fun meant kids.

Cedar Point Amusement Park day would begin with a huge breakfast in the church auditorium for the kids. The parents of the PTA made the breakfast and acted as chaperons at the park. Father rented three huge buses from Greyhound to take the kids to the park in Sandusky, Ohio. Father, somewhat of an artist, would make name tags for the children. He knew every one of their names by heart.

Father had one rule and that was to stay together in groups with the chaperones. Father would lead the way to the highest and scariest of roller coasters. It was never enough to ride the ride once. He would go multiple times until his stomach said "enough."

The rides were great, but he also loved the arcade full of games. He would play the race car game and take side bets with the kids to see who was the fastest driver of the group. He challenged a group of boys to a foosball game. The prize was a twenty dollar bill. Father would save up all year so he could give away money at the outings. It was out and out gambling, and he knew the bishop would frown on this. It would have been gambling if he actually won any of the games. He would purposely give up the lead so the children would beat him every time.

Father James treated the kids to all kinds of eats. He would buy them cotton candy, peanuts, hot dogs, ice cream, and everything in between. Father had a sweet tooth for taffy. He could finish a whole bag by himself. The kids would ride, play, and eat until way after dark. Father wore out the parents and kids. Father, still standing, said it was time to go. The new PTA parents thought he meant to go home. He said heck no. It was time to go wading in the lake. The camera flashed a picture of more than a hundred kids wading hand-in-hand in Lake Erie. Now it was time to go home. Tomorrow was Sunday, and he told the children he expected to see all of them at nine o'clock Mass.

Father James was the last to get home. Awaiting him on his desk was a letter from the bishop. The bishop wanted to see him first thing Monday morning concerning a criminal action brought against him. James went crazy all day Sunday trying to figure out what on God's good earth this "criminal action" meant. In frustration he visited Sister Angelus at the diocesan nursing facility she called home after breaking a hip. Good old Sister Angelus, now 102 years old, still had a sharp mind and would know what to do. Sister was shocked to hear that Father James was accused of a crime. Knowing Father James all these years, she just knew it was a mistake. Father reviewed his whole life with sister. He even told her about his personal sins. Some of his sins were downright funny to her. The end result was they couldn't find one thing in his fifty-five years of ministry that could be called criminal.

Monday morning broke dull and gray, reflecting Father's mood. He couldn't sleep that night and was at his ten o'clock appointment with the bishop a half hour early. The bishop's secretary greeted him cheerfully and with a cup of coffee. He didn't refuse the coffee, but he didn't drink it either. He just kept looking at his watch. The minutes crawled by, and after examining his conscience one last time, he decided to leave it up to the Lord.

Finally, he was summoned to the bishop's office. He timidly walked in. Bishop was sitting behind a desk five times bigger than his own. He was greeted by the bishop and another priest named Father Ronald. Ronald, sitting to the right of the bishop, was there to act as a witness to what was said. The meeting lasted twenty minutes. Twenty minutes that would forever change Father James's life. He was told a student had accused him of sexual abuse. He was told he could no longer be around children. He was told he could no longer say Mass. He was told to go to the same nursing home where Sister Angelus was living. He was told to make the move immediately. No inquest, no police involvement, no facing his accuser, and above all, no trial.

Father James obeyed.

Father's accuser was Father Gerald.

Epilogue

Joel's story about Father James was the last story to be told at Mader Hardware. The day before Joel's marriage to Jackie Eacott, the store was robbed. John closed the door for the last time that Friday night in June 1970. The next day the Maders celebrated the wedding at St. Benedict's Church. The following Monday the auctioneer was called. John secluded himself in the Manor Avenue home for two months. He lay in bed suffering from depression. Josef and Magdalena Mader died after celebrating sixty-four years of marriage. Magdalena died first, and Josef put his hand on her coffin and said, "Magdalena, keep the bed warm, I will see you in a little while." Stefan continued to walk past the vacant hardware store for another sixteen years. Joel would call him from time to time to see how he was doing. One day in the middle 1980s his phone went dead. It was said that Stefan still visited the asylum up until the day he died. Of all the storytellers, Stefan was the most gentle of men. Uncle Nicholas, the fiddle player, lived to be in his nineties. He loved to golf and told golfing stories into his late eighties. Joel last saw Uncle Nick boarding a plane to head home after his brother John's funeral. They shared one last drink together before takeoff. Stash and Larry, the fiddle bullies, became state legislators. Henry was killed in Vietnam. Charlie the cop became a tow truck driver later in life. He could never stop telling the "missing head" story to anyone who would listen. Milos, the sniper, died alone, and none of the storytellers attended his funeral. Father James died in the nursing home. He was a broken man who never tried to clear his name. No one knew or suspected that Father had been accused of the horrendous crime. The people of the parish were told he just retired and was ill and didn't want any retirement party.

As I walk through the family cemetery with my grandchildren, I point out the graves of our storytellers. I retell their stories to my grandchildren, hoping they will treasure them and tell them to their children.

CPSIA information can be obtained at www.ICGtesting.com
Printed in the USA
BVOW040031271112

306512BV00002B/10/P